ON A PEDESTAL

ON A PEDESTAL

R B Smedley

iUniverse, Inc.
New York Lincoln Shanghai

ON A PEDESTAL

iUniverse books may be ordered through booksellers or by contacting:

iUniverse
2021 Pine Lake Road, Suite 100
Lincoln, NE 68512
www.iuniverse.com
1-800-Authors (1-800-288-4677)

ISBN-13: 978-0-595-36665-1 (pbk)
ISBN-13: 978-0-595-81087-1 (ebk)
ISBN-10: 0-595-36665-1 (pbk)
ISBN-10: 0-595-81087-X (ebk)

Printed in the United States of America

CHAPTER 1

▼

There was an air of expectancy; excitement bubbled through the ranks of the workers gathered around the bunting bedecked platform. David Watson marvelled, not for the first time, at the emotions stirred by these occasions. After all, he reasoned, ship launches were not particularly unusual events on the River Clyde, probably the major shipbuilding area of the British Isles. A temporary wooden structure stood empty under the massive loom of the new hull's bow as the line of official cars slowly wound its way around cranes and other obstructions in the journey through the old shipyard. Watson watched the brightly coloured flags, secured to posts at each corner of the platform, shivering in the stiff breeze of the late summer afternoon. The sun was already low in the sky and he knew that the new hull soon to be launched would scarcely be tied up at the fitting out quay before nightfall. He looked up at the shipyard pennant flying so jauntily on a short mast at the bow of the hugely intimidating steel structure rearing above the crowd of shipwrights and engineers gathered to watch another ship launch. Viewed from ground level, the hull, neat and tidy in its primer paint, seemed, to the uninitiated, too unwieldy to float. David, for all his youth, was a veteran; he knew the partially completed vessel would look much smaller when it slipped into its natural element, particularly so without the yet to be fitted funnel and derricks.

The sponsor's car arrived opposite the steps leading up to the naming platform; a bowler hatted figure stepped forward to open the rear door and offer his hand to the as yet unseen occupant. David had heard a rumour that the sponsor would be the daughter of the shipowner whose vessel was due to be launched. He craned forward with his workmates, anxious to improve his view, then caught his breath in surprise. Stepping from the car was a young woman whose very presence seemed to transport him across the few yards separating them. Oddly she paused, one foot on the short staircase, and then turned to face the assembled throng. David became aware of a pale heart shaped face rimmed by dark, almost black, curly hair tossing rebelliously in the breeze. The woman hesitated briefly before being urged up the stairs by the man in the bowler. David could see that she was wearing a peach coloured dress of some soft flowing material that clung to her body, highlighting a slim, almost boyish figure. The hemline was perhaps shorter than fashion might have dictated but he appreciated the neat ankles and graceful calves as they ascended to the platform.

Almost immediately this vision was lost from sight as other important people pushed up the stairway to fill the platform. David assumed they were important although he didn't recognise anyone; tradition dictated that launching ceremonies were attended by shipyard directors with their wives together with members of the shipowner's family. Often someone from the House of Lords would attend in addition to local dignitaries. All the pomp associated with the launch of a new ship, despite the fact that this would be the twelfth such event he had witnessed since the start of his apprenticeship, never bored David. At 26 years of age his mind already sought adventures away from the confines and drudgery of the shipyard, from the squalor and hardship of wartime Clydeside in 1941. Yet on that September day he found himself wishing that he could be on the platform to catch another glimpse of the dark-haired young woman.

The general hubbub of the watching workforce sighed away and David heard a clear confident voice delivering firmly, in ringing tones, the time honoured phrases: "I name this ship *Petrain Castle*. God bless her and all who sail in her!"

There was the thump and tinkle of the champagne bottle smashing into the hard riveted plates of the ship's bow. David could imagine the restraining triggers being released, allowing Hull No. 140, now transformed by ceremony into the cargo vessel *Petrain Castle*, to begin her journey toward the welcoming waters of the River Clyde. He tensed, knowing that the next few minutes would be critical; it was not unknown for ships being launched to slew on the slipways causing serious damage and even physical injury. David's father had worked all night with his gang of shipwrights to ensure that the well-greased launchways were properly positioned, that every detail essential to a successful event had been attended to. He would be there now under the bow, David knew, making certain that the last of the holding chocks were hammered away, that the launch triggers had released.

A huge cheer went up from the gathered masses as, almost imperceptibly, the ship began to move. Bowler hats were held aloft on the naming platform; among them at the front David could see a long scarf-like strip of material waving. It was peach in colour and surely complemented the dress that had so caught his attention minutes earlier. The hull was moving more quickly now. It was possible to read the name, previously shrouded by large flags, proudly displayed in bold white letters along the bow just above the eye socket-like anchor hawse pipe. There was a heavy rattling sound as the first of the drag chains began to move. To control the speed of the accelerating steel mass several huge mooring chains had been attached to the hull, with their lengths flaked out in close-packed, carefully positioned loops to the side of the slipway. As more of the forged steel links began to move, the noise rose to a thunderous roar and the lower part of the ship became obscured by a rising cloud of dust and rusty flakes blasted off the unpainted chains.

Petrain Castle continued her plunge toward the river, constrained somewhat and no longer accelerating, yet still moving swiftly. Sliding straight and true, thought David happily whilst reflecting that the champagne bottle had shattered at the first attempt—always a good omen for a successful launch. There was a crash of water as the stern met the flat dirty surface of the Clyde. This was the critical instant when the vessel might begin to slew, but *Petrain Castle* was not going to spoil the day as she gracefully slid further until amid a maelstrom of disturbed water she was fully afloat. She sat there bobbing slightly, as if sampling the pleasure of flotation.

Then there was an explosion of congratulatory noise as the waiting tugs moved in to secure the ship and started hooting their steam whistles. Other ships in the vicinity of the shipyard joined in, all but blotting out the cheers of David and his workmates. The cacophony of sound lasted several minutes; then the tugs took command and the latest, still uncompleted, addition to the British merchant fleet was slowly towed away to the fitting-out quay. The yard workforce began to disperse but David hung on, waiting. He watched, fascinated, as the dark-haired sponsor, her face slightly flushed with the excitement of the occasion, returned to her car and was whisked away. *I wish I could meet someone like that,* he thought as he wandered through the shipyard, but, without consciously thinking about class barriers, he knew it was an impossibility: shipyard fitters simply did not meet shipowner's daughters. It would be some time before he would decide to change his situation.

The outfitting of *Petrain Castle* continued apace well into 1942, spurred on by the unfolding series of events in Europe: conflict with Germany having threatened for so long was now a two-year-old reality and the British Isles in their geographic isolation required every available merchant ship bringing in supplies to support the war.

For David Watson life had slipped into a blur of routine drudgery; after the excitement of the launch, an occasion he felt he would never forget, he had been working twelve hours a day installing and testing machinery throughout the winter. Leaving the house in the chilly pre-dawn darkness, then arriving back home in the evening after nightfall, exhausted by the hard physical demands of his job, he could do little more than eat dinner and collapse into bed.

The weekends were all too short, particularly if he was required to work an extra shift on a Saturday. In the usual course of events Tommy Waddington would come round expecting David to join him at the local football match. Occasionally they might cycle into Glasgow to watch Rangers play; David begrudged the money spent in getting through the football ground's turnstiles and really only accompanied Tommy out of a sense of loyalty to their friendship. Football was fine, thought David, but it might have been more interesting occasionally to go down to Gourock to watch the yachts racing. There was something about those craft that fascinated him: the surge of a sharp wooden bow cutting through the water, the crackle of taut canvas set against a stiff breeze, the squeal of blocks as sheets were freed during a tack—all served to excite his senses. Unfortunately yachting remained a rich man's sport, particularly so in wartime: he could only look on wistfully.

Curiously it was Tommy Waddington who made the suggestion that was to change David's life. With *Petrain Castle* nearing completion, the time for her Owner's acceptance trials approached. As fitters working on the vessel the two friends would be required to sail with her to tend the machinery, make minor adjustments or repairs as necessary whilst full speed trials along a measured mile were completed.

"I hear the owner's looking for junior engineers to sail with the ship on her maiden voyage," said Tommy casually one day, his thick accent almost incomprehensible to any but a fellow Clydesider.

"Aye," replied David unenthusiastically.

"Why don't we sign on then?"

"Don't be daft! Mah Mam and Dad would go crackers. Besides the buzz has it she's bound for South Africa; we'd be away for years."

But Tommy was not to be put off. "Mebbe, and after South Africa, who knows where next. What's wrong with a bit of adventure, eh?"

The two of them argued, without much heat, the pros and cons of the venture as they walked to the pub that night but without reaching any conclusion. As was usual on a Saturday evening, they met up with others from the shipyard in the Railway Arms for a few stiffening drinks before moving on to the local dance hall. Inevitably girlfriends past, present or potential were discussed, mainly in terms of whether they would 'do it' or not.

That particular Saturday David found himself stumbling through the last waltz with Eileen McFee as the evening drew to a close. Eileen had long had a crush on David and regarded herself at least unofficially as his girlfriend. She had to admit to herself, though, that he didn't appear to be especially committed to her. True, if he managed a dance or two, it was invariably with herself, but he never suggested they slip out of the dancehall to go round the back for a bit of kissing and who knew what. Not that Eileen McFee had any intention of going beyond kissing, she told herself sternly, but it would be nice to be asked.

For some reason Tommy's suggestion of the afternoon kept playing over in David's mind as they danced. Sensing some distraction in her partner, Eileen pressed her plump young breasts firmly against him.

"Penny for them," she said.

"What? Oh nothing," mumbled David.

"Something's bothering you," she persisted. "Come on, out with it!"

He regarded her thoughtfully, enjoying the pressure of her body, and then almost without thinking, blurted out, "Tommy wants us to go to sea."

Eileen was aghast. Was her man about to leave her, to go goodness knows where for who knew how long all without a second thought? She thrust herself even more fiercely against him as they continued to dance.

"You can't do it," she wailed. "What about us?"

David was shocked by the reference to 'us', having only told Eileen what Tommy had proposed in reaction to her probing; that there might be any 'us' to consider had not occurred to him. Suddenly, with a flash of insight, he saw his future stretching before him. A marriage to Eileen, or someone like her, then children and debts, trying to support a family: worst of all, he foresaw a lifetime locked into the shipyard for his livelihood. After all, what other means of earning a living that he could aspire to existed along the Clyde? The image repelled him. Without further thought he marched from the dance floor, a disconsolate Eileen trailing in his wake. He strode up to Tommy who was idly watching the dancers.

"Let's do it," he said without preamble.

For an instant his pal stared blankly, then beamed in understanding, "Right, you're on! Next Saturday morning…down the Owner's offices and sign on!"

Once the decision had been made, surprisingly, events fell neatly into place. David's parents accepted his decision, his mother philosophically and his father,

Angus, with some dark comment about it being better than conscription into the armed forces as the war progressed. The Shipowner's engineer superintendent, whilst not exactly welcoming the two of them with open arms, agreed to take them on provided they acquitted themselves satisfactorily on the upcoming sea trials of *Petrain Castle*. It was with some excitement that David looked forward to the acceptance voyage of the new merchantman.

CHAPTER 2

▼

The newly completed ship sailed proudly down the Clyde, her fresh paintwork glistening brightly on a cool yet sunny day. Of conventional design, *Petrain Castle* had a raised forecastle with a small deckhouse at the poop: a large accommodation block dominated the vessel amidships. The navigation bridge surmounted three deck levels of cabins, mess rooms and galley facilities set around the upper boundaries of the engineroom. A tall straight funnel, red painted with a broad black band at its upper edge, added imposing extra height behind the bridge. The ship was slightly unusual in layout because the owner had commissioned six extra cabins with a view to carrying a few passengers in addition to the general cargo she would carry in her four capacious holds. The sharp white cleanness of her painted upperworks contrasted with the solid blackness of her hull as she swept along.

Watchers on the shore, mainly from the families of shipyard workers, could see the builder's house flag fluttering stiffly at the masthead. It would remain there until the Owner was satisfied with his new ship when it would be replaced by the Shipping Line's colours in a ceremony indicating acceptance into service. A sharp-eyed observer might just have picked out David Watson lounging on the cargo hatch covers astern of the central superstructure; he was chatting with Tommy Waddington before the pair of them went down below to stand their engineroom watch.

"She's started off well enough," remarked David.

"Aye, none of the trouble we had with the winches on the last ship's trial," replied his companion. "Let's hope it stays that way."

"What do you reckon about the war? I hear there's lots of ships being sunk by submarines."

"Well, seems to me that's happening in the North Atlantic. If we go south we'll be fine. Anyway the Royal Navy will be there to protect us, sure enough." Tommy sounded a fraction less confident than his words might have suggested. Neither friend recognised the fallacy behind his words: the British Merchant fleet was being attacked in many areas, not just in the broad open spaces of the North Atlantic.

"You don't think the German submarines, them U-boats you hear about, will be a problem, then?"

The views of Tommy Waddington remained unexpressed as the two young men were summoned below for their engineroom watch. *Petrain Castle* turned from the river into the Firth of Clyde, her main propulsion engine running smoothly at close to full power. This large quadruple-expansion reciprocating steam engine dominated the centre of the cavernous white painted engineroom space, its piston rods flashing up and down rhythmically. Of open crankcase design, the rotating crankshaft in its huge bearings was frightening in its proximity. As David arrived on the steel plating at the lowest level, he could see the greaser of the watch checking the temperature of the bearings: a shoulder pressed firmly against a massive steel 'A'-frame engine support enabled the man, with a practised movement, to lift his hand slightly so as to touch the whirling bearing briefly as it whipped past within inches of his body. Dave wondered at the skill and confidence yet again, remembering that the first time he had seen the action he'd thought the greaser was out of his mind taking such risks. He still felt that a safer method could be devised but had come to accept that despite the inherent dangers the procedure was followed without injury at regular intervals each watch.

A second greaser was working at a higher engineroom level filling the oil boxes that fed the paired bearings where the thick piston rods drove the crankshaft through the huge connecting rods. In a much safer manner this man was also checking the bearings in his charge; as each piston rod surged to the full extent of its upward travel, he momentarily rested his hand on the cast brass bearing housing. David noted that the man seemed satisfied with each bearing until he came to the pair associated with the aftermost cylinder, the Low Pressure. The greaser felt the moving metal over several revolutions, shaking his head and applying extra oil from his long spouted can.

At length, the man whom David now recognised as Alf Tait slid down the steel ladder from his watch station to report to the Foreman in charge. David didn't need telling to know that there was a problem with the bearings. The normal hot oily smell of the engineroom was overlaid by a slight acrid taint in the vicinity of the Low Pressure Cylinder. It was a foreign unwanted stench, the sign of serious overheating. It would be necessary to slow down the engine, David guessed in order to let the damaged part cool.

Sure enough the Foreman moved to the voice pipe connected to the bridge. After a brief conversation complicated by the natural din of the machinery spaces, he strode across to the engine controls and began to close the main steam valve. Almost immediately, the main shaft, extending aft through watertight glands and supported by a number of bearings, began to slow. Alf Tait was back at his station pumping oil into the oil boxes in an attempt to cool and lubricate the damaged metal. Still the pungent aroma persisted.

The situation remained fraught for some while. The bearing continued to overheat though fortunately without worsening. The Foreman marched back and forth along the side of the slowly turning propulsion engine, frowning worriedly. Tait continued to fuss over the hot bearing. As testimony to the seriousness of the situation, the Shipyard Engineering Manager appeared in the engineroom to discuss matters with the Foreman. He left for the Bridge to advise the Pilot. It was essential that the ship stop in order that repairs could be undertaken.

"Get your spanners and scrapers ready, Watson," ordered the Foreman. "You too, Waddington. We'll be anchoring soon."

Within half an hour, *Petrain Castle* was safely moored in the lee of the Isle of Arran and authority was given to disable the engine. David and Tommy took it in turns with the heavy flogging hammers, releasing the bearing securing bolts and soon the damaged surfaces were exposed for repair. The two friends worked diligently under the watchful eye of the Foreman. When it came to reassembling the parts the lower half was replaced easily enough but the upper bearing cap jammed solidly on its securing bolts.

"Hang on, I'll wallop it," said Tommy, picking up the hammer.

Leaning over he supported himself with his left hand and swung the hammer with his right. There was a dull clang, then a thump as the bearing dropped into position. Tommy screamed in agony. David realised that the heavy brass object had trapped his friend's thumb, splitting the flesh. Blood flowed strongly mixing with the omnipresent oil to drip down over the connecting rod. It took some while to release Tommy and pack him off out of the engineroom for treatment. David stayed to finish the repair work before seeking out his pal.

"You're looking a bit under the weather, Tom. How come you hurt yourself...we've done bearings together often enough?"

A pale drawn, tired looking face smiled weakly from the bunk against which David was leaning. Waddington was hurting and having a hard time dealing with the pain despite having been given a strong sedative.

"Dunno, think me hand slipped when I swung the hammer."

"They tell me you're to be put ashore somewhere by Largs for treatment. Special boat coming out for you. How's it feel to be important?" said David somewhat at a loss as to how to comfort the other young man.

The one sided conversation fizzled out and David was glad when two of the shipyard riggers appeared with a stretcher. Tommy was strapped firmly to the stretcher, carried to the ship's side and gently lowered into a waiting launch. David waved a farewell, then made his way up to the bridge in order to report to the Engineer Manager.

It was accepted that Tommy's injury was an accident but not before David Watson and the Foreman had been carefully quizzed by each of a number of the Shipyard Managers gathered on the bridge. Watson was aware of two strangers in the gathering, one a middle-aged grey-haired man with a commanding presence, the other a thin non-descript individual. This latter David vaguely recognised as the Owner's engineer superintendent. In a flash of insight it occurred to him that the other person was most likely to be the Owner himself. He stared at the stranger, thinking that this must be the father of the young woman he had watched launch the ship the previous year. Dismissed from the bridge, he wandered down to the mess room in search of food, deep in thought, his mind flooding with recollections of that earlier and so important event in his life.

CHAPTER 3

▼

The sun was high and bright in a clear blue sky flecked with the occasional fluffy white cloud. The sea was calm yet governed by the long easy swell so typical of the mid-Atlantic Ocean on one of its quieter days. First trip Seventh Engineer David Watson sat in his favoured off watch position on the cargo hatch abaft the superstructure enjoying the peace of mind generated by the view. He listened to the hiss of disturbed water swishing along the sides of *Petrain Castle,* somehow managing to ignore the unrelenting rumble of machinery emanating from within the ship.

It was his first opportunity of the voyage to sit thus; the initial few days after leaving the Clyde had been hectic. He had had to adapt to a life dominated by a watchkeeping routine comprising four hours on duty followed by eight off. This was a regime that would control his life whenever the ship was at sea. Everything was a fresh experience for him. He was having to learn at a furious rate, not only his watchkeeper role in the engineroom but also how to make the adjustment to life at sea on a merchant ship. The tiny onboard community with its overlying chains of command remained something of a mystery to Watson. The Captain he perceived as some remote God-like figure rarely seen and never spoken to but whose word was law throughout the ship. David's own ultimate boss was the Chief Engineer, a muscular six-footer who did not keep a watch but was regularly seen about the engineroom inspecting his charge.

Dave had met "the Chief" on the day he had joined the ship. Knocking on the senior man's cabin door and opening it to enter, he had stood stock still just inside the room listening to the tail end of a conversation.

The Chief, obviously angered at something, had been in mid sentence, "…I'll have the bastard by the balls! Get him up here as soon as possible."

"Aye all right, Chief." The reply had been from his companion, a short wiry individual whom David was later to come to know as the Second Engineer.

David had rather self-consciously presented his brand new Discharge Book, the document that would become the record of his sea-going career.

The two men had turned to regard David somewhat suspiciously.

"First tripper?" the Chief had asked at length after a quick glance at the proffered paperwork.

"Yes, sir." David had been overawed by the sheer bulk of the man.

"Umm, well never mind," had come a reply that had sounded to Watson as though he were afflicted with some terrible, albeit curable, disease.

After the Second Engineer had taken his leave there had been a short interview that had left David bewildered as he stepped out of the cabin, really only aware that he was expected to join the Fourth Engineer on the eight o'clock to twelve watch. On the way to his cabin he had passed a short grimy looking individual with a rather hangdog expression clearly bound for the Chief's room. David had realised the man was probably the cause of the Chief's earlier anger. He had grinned broadly, struck by an image of the huge Engineer holding the unfortunate above his head suspended from a large fist clenching the man's testicles.

The Fourth Engineer, a cheerful, rather untidy man called Jim Terrier, was friendly and helpful to the inexperienced Watson. Indeed it was Jim's pleasant support that enabled David to make the necessary mental adjustment in order to be able to cope with life at sea. The original plan had been to ship out with his pal Tommy Waddington, two friends reacting together to a new challenge. Unfortunately the accident on the ship's trials had put paid to that scheme: the thumb would heal in time even if remaining slightly deformed but Tommy would not be fully fit for some months. Hence David was accepted for service on *Petrain Castle* without his friend. When he felt pangs of loneliness or homesickness he found that a laugh and a joke with Jim Terrier after their watch helped to dissipate his gloom.

Days aboard the freighter tended to follow an identical pattern: the watch-keeping grind, the unimaginative stodgy meals and the continual thunder of the engines all combined to induce a sense of routine boredom. Thus it was, after seven days at sea travelling in a small convoy on the maiden voyage bound for Cape Town, that great excitement was caused by a rumour of a radio message having been received that required a diversion to Gibraltar. The story spread amongst the crew like wildfire; any disturbance of the established routine was likely to create a stir—but for a ship to be sent into an unscheduled port was quite unprecedented, the old hands argued.

"Heard the rumour about Gib?" asked David casually, at the beginning of the watch.

"You don't believe that tripe do you?" replied Jim Terrier, somewhat condescendingly. "That's just the Second Steward inventing stories and trying to get us all going."

David hesitated. Terrier's words were a dash of cold water on his enthusiasm. He did not want the story to turn out to be a fabrication, but on the other hand he respected Jim's greater experience. As luck would have it, the matter was resolved within minutes as the sound powered telephone at the engine control station shrilled jarringly. It was the Chief Engineer. Jim listened attentively, nodding, somewhat superfluously, from time to time. He hung up with a "Right, Chief, will do."

Turning to David with a straight face, he said, "Chiefy wants No. 4 double bottom fuel tank pumped out; should be room in the cross bunkers, he reckons."

David, who normally handled any fuel transfers during the watch, set off toward the pump used for the duty, then stopped. "Why empty the tank now?"

"He wants to refill it," said Jim, struggling to avoid grinning at his partner's nonplussed expression. Finally, taking pity on his friend, he added, "to refill it in Gibraltar!"

"So it's true then!" shouted David. "Not some bright idea from the stewards. Great!"

The rest of their watch was interspersed with various discussions as to what they might do individually or together ashore in the foreign port.

At any other time the apes would have fascinated David Watson but he was too preoccupied to really appreciate them. For someone who had never even visited a zoo, the prospect of seeing the famous Barbary apes of Gibraltar at close quarters had seemed a must when he and Jim Terrier had been planning their off watch run ashore. An opportunely parked taxi driver had picked them up from just outside the dockyard gates and brought them to this spot high up on the Rock. If they had but known it, they were a trifle lucky to encounter a group of three animals that were happy to let the two engineers come close; indeed, Terrier was actually feeding an adventurous female from a bag of morsels provided by the taxi driver at modest cost.

Coming off watch at noon, the pair had had a hurried lunch on board before dressing to go ashore in a state of some excited anticipation. The change had come for David as they had approached the gatehouse at the entrance to the dockyard complex. Suddenly a large black Rolls Royce had swept past the gate-keeper, scarcely slowing to enable the driver to flash what David had taken to be some sort of pass at the startled official. As the vehicle had driven away he had caught a glimpse of the occupants; there had been two men in the rear seat but it had been the third passenger sitting alongside the driver that had caused him to stop and stare after the departing car. *Surely not!* he had thought. He had stood stock-still as the limousine had reached the bottom of the gangway of the distant *Petrain Castle.* The driver had scuttled around the car to open the door and out had stepped the young lady who had originally launched the ship. David had seen her quite clearly as she had marched confidently up the gangway accompanied by the two men.

Thus it was that he found himself watching apes eating and scratching themselves without really seeing them. His mind buzzed with the prospect of the young woman staying on the ship. Was she sailing with them? Why else would she have gone aboard? At least he now knew her name, surprisingly courtesy of Terrier. It was Megan Baxendell. A spiky sounding name, he thought, hoping that it didn't fit her personality too closely.

Eventually, Terrier having become bored with the apes, they climbed back into the taxi that swept them downhill, tyres squealing around the numerous curves, into the town of Gibraltar. Relaxing with a beer apiece in a small bar they had found in the main street, David casually brought the conversation around to Miss Baxendell.

"What do you think the Owner's daughter is doing on board, Jim?" he asked with a fair attempt at innocence.

Terrier smiled broadly, aware from the conversation he'd had earlier outside the dockyard when he'd volunteered her name, that David was smitten with the girl. "I dunno. Why—do you fancy her?"

David felt himself flushing but replied with studied casualness. "No, I was just wondering about having a passenger on the ship. Will we see her, maybe about the deck or in the saloon at mealtimes?"

"Don't you worry, she won't be interested in a couple of oily rags like us."

Scowling, David decided to let the subject drop sensing that his companion would not be particularly sympathetic. They had time for another glass of beer apiece before they had to return to the dockyard. Back on board *Petrain Castle* there was a bustle of activity as preparations were made to sail.

"That's odd," said Terrier, "looks like we're off again. I thought we were going to be here a couple of days at least."

Crossing the open deck, they were spotted by the Second Engineer who had been supervising the disconnection of the fuel bunker hose. "Come on you two, we sail at midnight."

"What's the rush, Sec?" called Jim.

"Captain's keen to be away."

For a moment David thought the Second Engineer was going to tell them that the Owner's daughter was on board and was in a hurry to be off.

"A U-boat was spotted in the Bay of Biscay by a Sunderland," continued their superior. "The Old Man thinks we'll be safer getting back to sea and heading south as soon as possible."

Privately, as he hurried along to his cabin, David felt they would all be better off staying in this major Royal Navy base. He had seen a variety of lean grey shapes berthed at the other side of the dockyard, cruisers and destroyers maybe, and felt very safe. But if the ship was sailing, so be it—David Watson was ready to stand his watch.

Petrain Castle sailed just after midnight, having spent less than twelve hours alongside; just enough time to take on fuel and some fresh provisions whilst leaving a few cases of whisky from the cargo for the garrison. As she sailed south one junior engineer dreamed about a particular passenger who for her part resigned herself to weeks of boredom on the way to South Africa.

CHAPTER 4

▼

The voyage south was only remarkable in its early stages for one major factor: it became increasingly hot and humid, particularly in the poorly ventilated engineroom. David Watson stood his watches with admirable stoicism, emerging on deck after his four-hour stint tired and dehydrated, his sweat-soaked boiler suit sticking to his glistening body. The excitement of Gibraltar had soon passed, overtaken by the grinding routine of tending the demanding, continuously turning, propulsion machinery. As Jim succinctly put it, "Drink gallons, take your salt tablets, grin and bear it!"

For David it might have been easier if he had been able to engineer a meeting with Megan Baxendell. He'd learnt through the ship's grapevine that she was travelling alone. Apparently she was a nurse and had been working in the large hospital on Gibraltar, but her father had pulled strings to have her transferred to the relative safety of South Africa. David was pleased that Megan's escorts had remained on the Rock. He had seen her, at a distance, on a couple of occasions strolling around the bridge deck, but that had been all. The Captain had taken the opportunity offered by having a passenger on board to take meals at different times to the junior officers. He'd taken to entertaining Megan in company with the Chief Officer, as well as the Chief and Second Engineers. Thus David had been deprived of the chance of seeing her in the Dining Saloon. Jim had mentioned that passengers on some ships were often shown around the engineroom as part of their cruise. David spent each morning watch for the first few days on passage in a state of excited expectancy. Gradually, however, he grew to accept that such a visit was unlikely.

It was possible that the situation would have remained unchanged throughout the voyage. Then, at twenty minutes past one in the morning when *Petrain Castle* was approximately 800 miles off Freetown on the African coast, fate took a hand. It was a clear moonlit night with little wind and a calm sea. The midnight watch change had left the Second Officer in charge on the bridge staring out into the darkness.

Abruptly the stillness of the scene was cruelly shattered by the dull crash of a heavy underwater explosion somewhere toward the bows. A huge fountain of water reared above the deck in line with No. 2 cargo hold and smashed down on the steelwork, spattering whitely. The Second Officer stood transfixed, unable to take in the messages his eyes were feeding his brain. Unchecked, the ship kept ploughing along her course, although there was a developing sluggishness in her motion as the sea began to flood the breached compartment. Finally accepting the calamity, the Officer rushed to take action, slamming the brass lever of the engineroom telegraph emphatically to the stop position. The telegraph bell tinkled; he could only hope the engineroom watch would be able to react swiftly to the command. He knew it would take some minutes to bring the machinery to a complete halt. There was no immediate "Stop" button. He prayed that the ship's forward momentum, coupled with the rapidly flooding hold, would not combine to force the bows under the surface of the sea. If that happened *Petrain Castle* would founder within seconds. There could be few survivors in that eventuality.

Captain Ellis stumbled across the coaming of the doorway at the rear of the bridge. In his haste he looked dishevelled and was still clad in pyjamas: they were red striped and he'd thrown his gold braided uniform jacket on also. He took in at a glance the telegraph set to "Stop" as he strode to the bridge window.

"She's down by the head already, Second."

"Aye, sir, thankfully the way's coming off her, though."

The rumble of the main engine had diminished noticeably, though the propeller shaft was still rotating slowly. In the engineroom the Third Engineer and his assistants dashed about shutting valves and gradually bringing the auxiliary systems back under control after the sudden telegraph order. Finally the engine was halted, *Petrain Castle* drifted to a stop and it was time to take stock of the situation. The vessel floated easily in the windless conditions. The bows were very close to the sea's surface but she seemed stable enough to Captain Ellis. Left alone, an unlikely event he conceded mentally, she would probably survive.

"Did we hit a mine, sir?"

"No, lad, it was a torpedo, I'm afraid. There will be more, likely enough. Yon German U-boat skipper will need to finish us off." Captain Ellis, a veteran of the

First World War, sounded resigned. "Better have the lifeboats run out ready to launch. Call all hands."

Shocked at the realisation that the ship had been attacked in an act of war, the young deck officer moved to obey.

As those on the bridge came to terms with the enormity of the emergency, so those below decks began to seek explanations for the explosion and the stationary engine. David Watson, ignoring the insistent clamour of alarm bells, charged along the alleyway from his cabin. Out on the deck he paused at the ship's rail. He was aware that all was not right with the freighter but was at a loss as to what to do. On a sudden impulse, he bolted up a nearby accommodation ladder, scrambled through a watertight door and found himself outside the Chief Engineer's cabin. He was about to knock when the door opened and his superior bustled past him.

"You'd best be off to your lifeboat station," rumbled the Chief as he strode past. "And don't forget a lifejacket!"

Still unaware that the ship had been torpedoed but beginning to accept the seriousness of the situation, David moved off to the starboard side of the ship toward No.2 lifeboat. As he did so he heard the clatter of feet on the stairway to the passenger deck above. He turned and almost collided with Megan Baxendell as she jumped down the last few steps. They stood staring at each other, neither immediately able to speak: she from breathlessness occasioned by her rush to find out why the ship was no longer moving and he as shyness froze his tongue.

Megan looked at the young man, sensing something familiar about him yet struck by the strength of his presence. She could see that he was good looking, fair haired and broad shouldered, but it was his eyes that made her heart skip a beat. Their greyness was calm, seeming to radiate security and a sense of purpose. With an effort she looked away.

"What's happening?" she managed at length.

David for his part was still recovering from the shock of coming, finally, face to face with the young lady who had so impressed him at the launch of *Petrain Castle* all those months ago.

"Er, I'm not sure," he replied lamely, seeing the flicker of disappointment cross her flawlessly complexioned features. "But the Chief told me to get along to the lifeboat," he added quickly. "I'm sure you should do the same. At least until we know what's what."

They made their way out onto the boat deck. The area was buzzing with activity as crewmembers began to gather from around the ship. To add to the noise of alarm bells, a boiler safety valve vented with a sharp crack and a huge gush of vapour from the funnel as it relieved the excessive steam not required by the stopped engine. The Third Officer was already organising a party of sailors to remove covers, release the gripes and ready the lifeboat for launching. David crossed to a large locker set against the white painted deckhouse. Delving inside, he emerged with two rather grubby white life jackets. He handed one to Megan, then helped her put it on correctly, finally tying it in place firmly. As he did so he felt her shiver in the cool night air, the thinness of her blouse scant protection. Without thinking he slipped off his uniform jacket with its single thin stripe of rank on each sleeve and draped it around her shoulders. Megan made no comment but clutched it firmly about her body in gratitude. He sensed her warm smile in the darkness.

A voice boomed from above: "How's it going Three-Oh?" It was the Captain on the wing of the bridge. "Let me know when you're ready to launch—there's a German submarine out there just waiting to hit us with another torpedo."

Further conversation was abruptly stifled as a dull report followed by a loud screeching, tearing noise assailed their ears. Before David could work out that a gun was being fired, the same succession of sounds was repeated. This time they were completed by a heavy crash somewhere on the front of the bridge. Debris from the impact of the shell hurtled overhead. A vicious shard of metal whirred to silence with a soft thud. A sailor standing on the lifeboat gunwale coughed, then almost gracefully pitched over backwards. As the man fell into the sea, he died without even knowing that he had been struck by a shell splinter. The realisation of danger suddenly gripped the group gathered at the lifeboat. Men ducked and dived for cover as David pulled Megan into shelter beside the life jacket locker.

They tensed for another impact on the ship but the hidden gun stayed silent. Instead a voice shouted from the darkness. The English was not clear but its authority was implacable: "Do not use your radio again or I will continue to fire!"

David peered out into the night but could see no sign of the attacking U-boat. The dim moonlight would be highlighting *Petrain Castle* but the German commander was cleverly keeping his vessel hidden from sight. Not that there was any risk to exposing himself: the cargo ship was unarmed.

"I think we're going to be leaving soon," said David in a mood of irony.

Megan looked at him questioningly for a moment. Then her face cleared. "You mean, abandoning ship?"

There was a sharp nod of the head as he moved back toward the lifeboat. Instinctively she followed closely. The Third Officer reappeared, having decided that the danger from the gun had receded, at least temporarily. He gave orders for the lifeboat to be swung out on its davits and lowered to deck level ready for embarkation. Without warning the ship's steam whistle started to sound a continuous succession of deep sonorous notes.

"That's the 'Abandon Ship' signal," murmured David to his companion. "Nice to know someone survived that shell into the bridge."

It was apparent that the decision to abandon had been based mainly on the unseen yet palpable threat posed by the U-boat. *Petrain Castle* remained stable, on an even keel albeit noticeably down by the bows. It seemed to Watson that she was in a fairly stable condition.

The Third Officer ordered the assembled group into the waiting boat, remaining by himself at the winch brake ready to lower. David helped Megan take a seat on a thwart toward the stern of the wooden vessel but did not immediately step aboard.

"Don't worry, you'll be quite safe. I'll be back after I've given the Third Mate a hand."

When everyone had embarked except for David and the Third Officer, the latter eased the brake to allow the lifeboat to descend. Almost immediately it stopped moving, juddering to an uneven halt some eighteen inches below its starting point. In the weak moonlight David could see a host of upturned faces all showing concern over the unexpected stoppage.

"Give us a hand, Dave," called the Third Officer. "The damned brake's jammed again; I can't get it to release."

There had been problems with the brake in earlier tests, which was the reason David had hung back. Despite overhaul, the equipment had shown an occasional unpredictable penchant for sticking. The two men heaved at the release arm ineffectually and with increasing frustration. They were joined by the Chief Engineer who, although mustered to be in the Number One lifeboat, had noticed the problems being experienced with Number Two.

"Let me have a look at it," he growled. David and his companion stepped back respectfully. The senior engineer shrugged off his reefer jacket and handed it to David. Then, somewhat to his surprise, the Chief released from its securing bracket the handle used to operate the winch when recovering the lifeboat to its storage position. "Let's try some old fashioned percussive persuasion," he said with a grin." Then, hefting the heavy steel handle like a hammer, he slammed it sharply a number of times into the side of the brake casing. The last impact induced a loud metallic click from the offending item. The lifeboat slipped a further few inches on its wire falls.

"That should do it—now get yourselves aboard. I'll take over here."

The note of authority in the man's voice did not allow of any argument although the two young men he was addressing knew it was not the Chief Engineer's responsibility to be launching the lifeboat. Obediently, therefore, the pair jumped down onto a thwart, settling themselves into a seated position as their conveyance gradually descended to the surface of the sea. David looked up as the lifeboat came afloat and was released from its falls; he could see a white shirted arm waving farewell as the Chief Engineer moved off to join the group boarding the Number One craft. It was only then that he realised that he was still holding the Chief's uniform jacket. He shrugged, thinking that he would return it when the other boat was safely away from the ship. In the meantime he slipped his arms into the sleeves and drew the coat around himself, glad of the extra warmth.

With the Third Officer seated at the helm, the lifeboat was rowed slowly away from *Petrain Castle*. In the distance it was just possible to make out the second craft pulling away in a slightly different direction. After a while the boat was stopped and everyone settled down to wait for the dawn due in a couple of hours time. The Third Mate's plan was to link up with their shipmates in Number One before heading toward the African coast. David had moved into a space next to Megan: it seemed quite natural that she should snuggle against his shoulder and doze lightly. In different circumstances he would have felt very happy but the inherent dangers of their situation left him more concerned than pleased.

They were stirred from their somnolence abruptly by the spiteful bark of the U-boat's gun firing. This time David saw the orange flash of the muzzle with the fuzziest of images behind it; a dark structure, the conning tower, topped by a black figure wearing a white-topped cap. A huge crashing explosion diverted his attention back to *Petrain Castle*. Gouts of bright flame spurted from a large hole in her side adjacent to the engineroom. More shells rained in on the doomed vessel. It was apparent that she was to be sunk by gunfire. Each round was accurately placed close to waterline. She began to settle perceptibly. The gun stopped firing. In an excellent piece of judgement, the German had hit her sufficiently to ensure the sinking without wasting ammunition.

David found himself hugging Megan hard as the ship that he'd helped build slowly began to sink deeper by the bow. He felt immensely saddened, as if a small part of him were dying with the once fine vessel. The stern rose higher in the water until the huge bronze propeller was scarcely immersed. Oddly, the movement ceased with the great steel hull poised in some strange position of balance. Then there was a noise of machinery breaking loose in the unnatural attitude followed by a massive whooshing report from forward as the failure of a major bulkhead signalled the beginning of the end. With ever-increasing velocity *Petrain*

Castle plunged beneath the surface. The water disturbance subsided: she was no more.

There were tears on David's cheeks as the reality and finality of it all bore in on him. Megan saw his dismay, yet there was more—she felt the distress boiling within him. She was left to wonder as David sat holding her, silently looking out across the sea that was once again smooth.

CHAPTER 5

▼

The grey slivers spreading across the darkened horizon announced the coming dawn. In the coolness before the sun's arrival, a sleepless David Watson found himself searching for the second lifeboat. Alongside him on the thwart Megan stirred from a light sleep. They had talked a little during the night: about Megan's visit to South Africa, about David's career at sea, and about their respective families. They had been happy and relaxed in each other's company. He looked down at her dark curls rested against his shoulders and smiled.

"How do you feel?" he asked quietly.

"Umm, I'll be fine I think." The comment carried little conviction.

"Don't worry, we'll be ashore in Africa soon. Besides, the Navy will be looking for us before long. Maybe we got a radio message off before the shelling started." David felt the need to be supportive and struggled to inject an element of confidence into his voice. Privately he admitted to himself that he was worried. There was no indication as to how far distant the African coast lay. He looked across at the Third Officer, speculating as to that worthy's navigational abilities.

The light strengthened gradually; it promised to be another fine day. David fervently hoped it would hold less of the unexpected than the previous one. His hopes were about to be dashed.

"There they are, Three-Oh," called a raucous voice from the bow of the boat.

Everyone strained their eyes in the direction of an outstretched arm. Sure enough, the second craft drifted in the calm sea, perhaps a mile or so off to the port side. But she was not alone. Towering over the defenceless little boat reared the black bulk of the German submarine's conning tower. The U-boat seemed to be actually alongside the wooden vessel.

"What are they doing?" asked a voice.

"Maybe the bastards are going to sink the boats as well as the ship," came a strained squeak of a reply.

"Look! There's someone going aboard the bloody sub!"

Sure enough, a large figure could be seen being dragged from the lifeboat onto the casing of the U-boat. The man was hustled away through a hatch into the interior of the warship. A hazy puff of bluish grey smoke rose into the air; there was a flurry of disturbed water at her stern and the submarine surged purposefully ahead. She turned and it became apparent that she was moving toward them. As the dawn light strengthened still further they could see armed sailors gathered at the base of the conning tower. They watched, worried but bereft of any ideas for action.

The black steel loomed alongside; they could hear orders being passed in a guttural tongue as the vessel slid to a halt. A face stared at them, seemingly searching. A hand pointed. "You, come aboard, now!"

There was some confusion in the lifeboat as to whom the German was indicating. A man David recognised as the Bosun resolved it.

"I think he means you, lad," he said.

David was horrified yet still disbelieving.

"What could they want with *me*?"

The uncertainty was set aside when a burly German sailor pointed a rifle directly at David and shouted, "*Komm!*"

There was no mistaking the raised gun barrel and David stood up slowly. He felt a small warm hand grasp his and squeeze tenderly. He looked down into the liquid brown eyes of Megan: they were filled with concern and something close to a tear. He gathered strength from the contact although she did not speak.

"I'll be fine and so will you be. Good Luck!"

As he moved across the loaded lifeboat he paused for an instant, then looked back at her. "See you in London," he said with a grim smile. Later he would wonder what impulse had extracted those words from his mind. On the face of it the statement was fatuous, given the circumstances, but he knew that he had meant it and believed it would happen.

He was helped over the gunwale and onto the casing of the waiting U-boat. Megan watched hopelessly as he was whisked through a steel door in the base of the conning tower and out of sight. She felt tears running down her cheeks and turned away to hide her face. A rumble of machinery announced the departure of the submarine. Wiping her eyes quickly she glanced back at the vessel: two hard eyes seemed to spear her from under a white-topped cap. The German captain, for she was sure it was he, lifted a hand in a half wave then swung away. Within minutes the warship was gone, disappearing into an early morning haze.

Sensing the despair that enveloped the boat, the Third Officer spoke out. "Come on lads. I don't know what all that was about, but its past history now. Let's get over to the other boat—find out what they have to say."

There was some adjustment to the seating positions in the lifeboat as the oars were extracted from their stowage position under the thwarts. Megan found herself being shunted aft to sit alongside the deck officer in the stern. After a period of familiarisation with the long sweeps, they got under way and steered for the second vessel.

"Ahoy there, what are your intentions? Is Captain Ellis aboard?"

"Come alongside!" called a voice that turned out to be that of the Chief Engineer. The crew of the Number One craft looked as shocked and demoralised as those of their compatriots. They sat with heads bent and Megan could see that they had not yet made any attempt to ship the oars. The senior engineer and the young deck officer discussed the situation: it turned out that the Captain had been taken aboard the U-boat and the Chief Officer had been wounded during the shelling. He could be seen stretched on the bottom boards, a hasty bloodied bandage swaddling his upper left arm.

"It's not too bad: we've stopped the bleeding. I think it's mainly shock, but the sooner we get him ashore the better," said the Chief.

"What about the Second Mate?"

"I'm afraid he was killed along with Sparks in the shelling."

The Third Officer felt the colour drain from his cheeks; normally the Second would have been in charge of the Number Two lifeboat but had remained on the bridge at the Captain's request. If the torpedo had struck two hours earlier it would have been he, the Third, who would have remained on the bridge as part of his watch. The closeness, the reality of death felt almost tangible. He shook his head in disbelief at the vagaries of fortune.

"Why did they take Captain Ellis?"

"I'm not sure—probably think we'll have problems manning ships in the future without competent skippers. If his ship had been bigger, maybe the damned German would have imprisoned the whole bunch of us!" replied the Chief. "Who did they take from your lot?"

"Dave Watson."

"That's odd. I wonder why him of all people."

In a flash of insight the reason came to Megan. "I think it may have been a mistake."

The two officers looked at her oddly.

"What do you mean, lass?"

"The Germans thought he was yourself, Chief."

"And why would they think that?"

"The uniform—he was wearing your jacket!"

"Good Lord, I do believe you could be right." The Chief couldn't help a chuckle at the thought. "I bet young David won't be too pleased by his early promotion. Let's hope the Germans aren't too put out when they find out the truth."

"What do we do now, Chief? Hang around and wait for rescue or make for Africa?" The Third Officer was impatient to be moving.

"The German skipper gave us a course to steer for the coast." He passed across a scrap of paper. "I suggest we stay in company and follow that direction."

The two lifeboats set off in line astern with long easy strokes of the oars. With little or no wind there would have been little point in setting the small lugsails although both had their short masts stepped in preparation. Progress through the day was slow and to some on board the boats the exertion seemed pointless. After hours of effort the seascape had not changed: the same flat surface, the same blue sea, the same pitiless sun beaming from a cloudless sky all combined to give the impression that they had not moved. Toward dusk, however, the weather began to change as a slight breeze blew up. There was a shouted exchange between the two craft and they closed on each other, eventually running a line between the stern of one and the bow of the other. They lay thus drifting slowly through a difficult night. It remained hot and humid, the variable wind seeming to lack all cooling effect. There was an acceptable supply of water in the storage tank but the Third Officer, wisely in Megan's opinion, had instigated a strict rationing regime from the outset. They were each issued half a cup of water with every meal. It was something of an exaggeration, she felt, to term two biscuits, some chocolate and a handful of milk tablets a *meal* but she was grateful for the sustenance nonetheless.

At dawn, having slept fitfully, Megan shook away the remnants of a strange yet quickly forgotten dream and studied the horizon. There was nothing to be seen; no ships rushing to their rescue, no landfall, simply an unending blankness. Somehow she had assumed that their ordeal would not last for long. This was clearly not the case and the harsh reality of it struck her hard. For a moment her head sank down to her chest in a gesture of defeat but somewhere inside a little spark still glowed. She remembered David's parting words and with them came a feeling of resolve. "Head up and face the world," she whispered to herself. The sea remained as featureless as ever yet somehow it did not seem quite so depressing.

She looked outward again; the two boats separated and with mutual agreement hoisted their sails. The wind from a fickle variable annoyance had settled into a helpful westerly. They rolled along happily in the slight swell, the breeze raised, making good distance in the required direction. It was apparent that the Number One boat was slower than its twin, possibly because it carried more passengers. The distance between the two tended to increase and Megan was conscious of the Third Officer's efforts to slow their craft in order to maintain station.

"Would you like to try your hand at the tiller, Miss Baxendell?" asked the deck officer. "I need to sort out breakfast."

"Please, it's Megan."

He smiled, "Okay, Megan it is and I'm Richard—Dick if you like—Rafferty. Now take hold of the tiller. See the compass? Try to hold the compass needle in more or less the same place."

They discussed the mechanics of sailing the big heavy dinghy and Megan assimilated the basics of holding a steady course. After a while she began to enjoy herself, feeling the response of the craft to her movements of the tiller. Once he became satisfied with her efforts, Rafferty busied himself with dividing up their meagre supplies to give each of the twenty-one occupants of the lifeboat some sustenance. The morning turned out to be an almost pleasant experience for Megan. She proved to have a natural aptitude for sailing and Rafferty was happy to leave her to it. There were clouds in the sky now and occasionally they were shielded from the sun's direct glare by this cover. Her discomfort caused by sweat and a general unwashed feeling was put to one side temporarily as they swooped over the waves.

The wind continued to rise through the day and by late afternoon Rafferty began to look regularly astern with a worried frown on his face. Megan forbore from asking him why he looked concerned. She could work out his reply for herself. That evening the two boats came together again, having dropped their sails. This time, however, the increased swell made it risky to deploy the linking rope. The First Officer seemed to have recovered somewhat as she could see him in the stern of Number One, his good arm hooked over the tiller. As the night dropped quickly around them like some gigantic cloak, she could hear singing from their neighbours as they endeavoured to keep their spirits up.

"Do you know how far to the coast, Dick?"

The Third Officer looked thoughtfully, then, as though coming to a decision, said quietly, "I can't be sure, of course, but from what I remember of the chart I would guess we're something like 800 miles from the coast of Africa."

Megan was stunned. The shock showed on her face and Rafferty peered at her with concern.

Finding her voice at last she tried to make sense of the information: "But that must be weeks away!"

"Well, maybe a couple. Hopefully less if the wind holds out."

As the night drew on the weather began to deteriorate. The wind strength increased: it was no longer a benign helpful influence. It began to whip the tops off the ever-taller waves. Spray soaked everyone in the boat. Megan, hunched in misery at the stern, pulled David's uniform jacket tighter around her and silently blessed him for giving it to her. The thought jolted her and she wondered how he was finding life on a foreign warship.

The two lifeboats rapidly separated although in the darkness it was not immediately apparent. The singing had ceased some hours previously when Rafferty shouted out to where he thought the other boat might be: there was no response and he steeled himself to accept that they were alone. Nothing could be done about the separation in the darkness and by morning Number One could be anywhere. It was a long cold night for the young man, worried by the weather, frightened at the possibility of being alone at daybreak.

At dawn the horizon was clear—Number One had indeed vanished. The weather continued to cause concern. It was not a full-blown storm but Rafferty knew it still represented a considerable risk factor. It would put a heavy strain on his boat handling skills. He nudged Megan awake.

"We need to put up some sail. Hopefully it'll stabilise the boat…make it steadier, safer. Would you take the tiller, please? She'll come into the wind as we hoist. Just hold her there, if you can!"

He moved forward, shaking a couple of sailors awake in his passage. Megan watched as they readied the lugsail for rehoisting. She could see Rafferty making knots in lengths of cord around the boom. At length the men seized the halyard and began to haul the sail up the stubby mast. Immediately the wind caught the first fragment of canvas, ruthlessly dragging the boom and the remaining sailcloth across the boat. The three men ducked as the spar scythed from one side to the other. The motion caused the boat to pivot but she countered instinctively with a twitch of the tiller. The boat stabilised as the sail was finally sweated home. It crackled loosely in the wind, its restraining sheet thrashing loosely. She could see that the sail was much smaller than on the previous day, the excess having been strapped to the boom.

Rafferty stumbled aft and it was only then that she realised he was hurt. One side of his face was streaked in blood, spread by the salt spray into a hideous mask. Megan stretched forward and grasped his arm, guiding him back into his seat.

"Bloody silly of me, should have looked out for the swing of the blasted boom," he offered weakly by way of explanation.

She could see a nasty gash just below the hairline oozing slightly; it was probably not too serious, she guessed, provided it was kept clean.

"Here, you steer," she said, then set about tending the wound. There were no medical supplies in the boat so she contented herself with ensuring it was clean, then bound it with strips torn off her skirt.

"You look like a pirate," she said at length, leaning to one side to examine her handiwork.

"Thanks! At this moment you look like Florence Nightingale to me," replied Rafferty with a broad grin.

"Well, there's obviously not much wrong with you!"

The lifeboat ploughed along in a cloud of spray throughout the morning. Megan shared the helming duties with her companion, musing on the accident that had split Rafferty's head open. It occurred to her that all of them in the boat were heavily dependent for their future on the young man at her side. She surveyed the faces in front of her; there were none she recognised, of course, but she knew that most of them were from the engineroom, greasers, stokers and such. There would be sailors amongst them as well, she knew, but there were no other deck officers who could sail and navigate the craft as far as she could see. She based her thoughts on uniforms. All officers wore a navy blue jacket with insignia of rank on the sleeve. She instinctively glanced at the thin gold band on the sleeve of her borrowed coat.

Although Megan was not aware of it, there were engineer officers in the boat who were attired in boiler suits, not having had time to change after the torpedoing. She was, however, entirely correct in her assumption that they were all heavily reliant on the skills of Third Officer Rafferty—skills that would be heavily tested in the days ahead.

CHAPTER 6

▼

"You know, Captain Ellis, I don't know how they put up with this for long periods," said David Watson with feeling, staring around the space.

He was voicing the feelings they had both shared since coming aboard. They were seated on a spare torpedo in the forward torpedo room of the German submarine *UB-132*. The area was in fact their prison although they were free to move around within it; after a week aboard they were both heartily sick of their confinement. David was particularly bothered by the lack of space to exercise. True, they were each allowed time on deck every night when the U-boat surfaced to charge its batteries: but for one hour's fresh air they had to endure a further twenty three cooped up in the claustrophobic torpedo space.

"It's the smell that gets me, lad," replied Hubert Ellis. "Do you mind the first time they brought us below?"

An operational submarine always suffers from trapped odours and *UB-132* was no exception. Her characteristic stench, and there was no better word to describe it, was a mixture of human body smells and the taint of cooking dominated by the sourness of boiled cabbage. This olfactory melange was heavily overlaid by the strong smell, indeed at times it seemed almost the taste, of diesel oil. The stink had hit them as they had entered the conning tower when being escorted through the submarine. It remained with them for as long as they stayed aboard the U-boat: it was something they would not easily become accustomed to.

"How long will we be kept on board, I wonder?" murmured David.

"If I were the commander I would be only too happy to be rid of us," replied Ellis. "After all, we must affect his operational readiness somewhat."

David frowned. "Yes, I suppose we're in the way and consuming rations as well."

"He was obviously acting on orders when he took us aboard. Unfortunately, the damned sub seems to be nearer the beginning of its patrol than the end, judging by the number of torpedoes still stored in this space. Either that or they haven't had many targets," went on the old Captain. A large grey haired individual running somewhat to fat, Ellis was more phlegmatic in their situation than his younger companion.

The two men had only met the U-boat's skipper briefly just after their capture. He had quizzed Captain Ellis carefully about *Petrain Castle*, her cargo and destination, but the questioning had scarcely become an interrogation. It seemed the man was simply seeking details for his logbook. For his part, Ellis was only prepared to confirm the name of his past command, remaining silent about the cargo. Curiously Watson was merely asked for his name, which he was happy to divulge, and so his true rank remained hidden from the German.

The conversation between the sturdy old Captain and the young engineer continued as a desultory debate centred on their chances of an early release from *UB-132*. It was as much a way of filling in time as anything else, but suddenly their discussion was interrupted by an alarm klaxon filling the boat with its raucous tones. There was the sound of feet pounding along steel walkways, more men pushed into the torpedo room and then the watertight door at the entrance to the space was slammed shut. The sound of the steel retaining dogs being applied to the door had an air of finality about it that David found unnerving. The sense of claustrophobia increased.

Orders were being given as the Germans deployed to their battle stations around the space. A petty officer picked up a sound powered telephone and reported to the control room. There was silence in the area aside from the background hum of machinery at the after end of the submarine. David realised that the U-boat had found another target and was probably stalking it at that very moment. The German seamen remained alert but inactive for what seemed an age. There were occasional guttural discussions on the telephone until, abruptly, there was a sharp loud gush of compressed air followed by a dull thump. The sound was repeated. David was aware of the flow of water in a pipe near his head.

"That'll be the compensating ballast," whispered Ellis. "They need to balance the weight lost when the torpedoes are fired or the sub will change depth, maybe even break the surface."

David nodded in acceptance although he wasn't sure that he fully understood what was going on. There was an air of expectancy in the torpedo space: the Germans stood quietly, apparently listening. Then there was the unmistakable sound of a distant explosion; a second dull bang was heard, then the seamen began cheering and slapping each other on the back. David realised he had just heard the destruction of another fine ship. He found himself hoping that her crew would be able to abandon without injury.

The attitude of the submarine changed as the bow rose. David guessed they were about to surface. There were more compressed air sounds, more water flow as *UB-132* clawed her way toward the surface. The vessel levelled out. From the distance came the clang of a hatch being flung open, then another. Although he could not see, David imagined the German commander in his peaked white-topped cap standing in the bridge area at the top of the conning tower whilst the gun's crew assembled around their weapon on the foredeck. His thoughts were interrupted as more telephone orders were received.

"Ve reload now! Ready next Britisher, ja?" a small wiry sailor smiled at the two prisoners.

They knew him as Larsen and had developed a relationship with him in the previous week. This was largely based on the fact that the man was the only person with any knowledge of English in the torpedo room. Larsen was almost friendly and had made it his duty to ensure the two prisoners received food and water. He turned away obviously pleased with the U-boat's success in action and was soon embroiled in the mechanics of reloading the emptied torpedo tubes.

Ellis nodded toward the activity. "At least it will give us a bit more room!"

The spare missiles were stored on racks at the sides of the space. These racks were almost full but with two removed to their firing tubes the main advantage would be extra area for sleeping.

For some time the U-boat could be felt to be manoeuvring and David assumed that she was getting in to position from which to shell her prey. He was proved wrong when two new faces joined them.

"Bang goes the extra legroom," observed Ellis dryly as he stretched forward to welcome the new arrivals.

It was obvious that they were also prisoners although their uniforms were somewhat different.

"Hello! Welcome to the South Atlantic cruise liner, *UB-132*. I'm Ellis, until recently skipper of *Petrain Castle* and this is Dave Watson."

"Jan Klijn, Captain, *M/V Talag* and Hans Gaiger. Pleased to meet you." The Dutchman gave a half bow, repeated by his companion after a brief pause. The English was heavily accented but precise. Klijn was a short rotund individual, normally happy and smiling but for now his face was grimly scowling.

"They haf sunk my ship and killed many of my crew. Two torpedoes…one in the engineroom…all dead."

"We were luckier, most of my lads got away in the boats," replied Ellis sympathetically.

The two skippers began discussing the loss of their respective commands whilst their erstwhile subordinates talked about life as prisoners on a patrolling German U-boat. The mention of lifeboat survivors stirred David to wonder how Megan was getting on: he earnestly hoped she was faring well.

By sheer coincidence *UB-132* was not very far from the Number Two lifeboat of *Petrain Castle*. The submarine's patrol had taken her south, then east after sinking the British ship. As she turned and headed north again, Dick Rafferty was resolutely steering his tiny command eastward just out of sight of the U-boat's starboard lookout. After a week of brisk winds they had made good progress toward the distant African coastline. The sailing had been reasonably easy and he had been greatly assisted at the tiller by Megan. There was no way that he could estimate their position, being without chart or navigation instruments but he was heartened by the knowledge that following the same easterly course must bring them to shore. As he'd joked with some of the sailors, even he couldn't miss as big a lump of land as Africa.

For her part Megan had settled to the routine of the tiny community of the lifeboat. She had learnt to put up with the physical privations; the feelings of perpetual hunger were perhaps the worst, although the painful sunburn made movement something of a torture. The sailing of the lifeboat before the wind was something of a bonus. She found herself thoroughly enjoying her stints at the tiller. It was as though life was offering her a balance: the pleasures of sailing to offset the hardship of surviving on the boat. It occurred to her that they had been extremely lucky since the torpedoing. The mood in the boat had become cheerful once the initial shock of the torpedoing had worn off. It remained so, helped no doubt by the obvious progress they were making. Generally the health of the survivors was fine despite the lack of real sustenance. Her only concern was for Dick Rafferty; he had survived the blow to his head with no indication of concussion but the scalp wound had not healed, as she would have expected. She cleaned it every day but the salt water seemed to be interfering with the normal healing process. The edges of the cut were inflamed and she could tell that he was running a slight temperature. For some unexplained reason the lifeboat's medical box was missing. There was therefore no antiseptic available with which to treat the young man. Megan realised that she could do nothing other than try to keep the wound clean but she fretted knowing how much they all depended on the young officer.

On the evening of the ninth day their luck started to run out. The weather decided it had been helpful for long enough. The wind disappeared entirely. For more than thirty hours they wallowed, totally becalmed. There was not a cloud in the sky. The sun was pitiless, baking the survivors as if in an oven. Tempers began to fray as their morale was roasted out of them. Dick confided to Megan that there might be fights over the water and food ration if the heat persisted.

"God forbid it comes to a scrap!" he said. "We'll never make it ashore if the rationing isn't adhered to."

She looked at him. The strain was beginning to show. His face was haggard, his skin pale below his head bandage. His shoulders were hunched in an attitude of defeat. Megan laid her hand on his arm and squeezed reassuringly.

"Come on," she said quietly. "Remember, you said we would be ashore in two weeks from the sinking. We've done most of that time; just keep going a few more days and we'll be safe."

He smiled weakly but said nothing.

"Get some sleep," she encouraged. "I'll wake you if the wind returns."

Rafferty slept, although whether it was true sleep or feverish unconsciousness Megan was not sure. From time to time she placed her fingers on his forehead. It was burning hot. She sat in the stern sheets of the lifeboat supporting the weight of her companion, thinking about his sickness. There had been no reason to mention that she was in fact a trained nurse and had only left Gibraltar at the express instruction of her father who had feared that the German Army might attack the Rock from Spain. Her formal training only compounded her fears for Rafferty's well-being. She decided to keep the reality of his condition to herself as long as possible. There was enough unrest among the overheated survivors without them being aware of their leader's frailty.

Finally the wind returned, but from a different direction. Previously they had bowled along under the impetus of a following westerly in ideal sailing conditions. The new breeze was from the south, catching the lifeboat on the side and tending to roll it so that the gunwale came perilously close to the surface of the sea. Rafferty was awake and lucid though still carrying a worrying temperature. He adjusted the sail to the wind, then ordered the occupants of the boat to move where possible to bring more weight to the windward side. This had the desired effect as they settled again to a more or less even keel. There was, however, a rolling motion now that hadn't been there before and Megan felt an inherent instability in the new situation.

Rafferty demonstrated a noteworthy skill as a sailor in the fresh wind. It was not easy coping with a gusty breeze that was imparting a heavy rolling motion along with its forward drive, but he seemed to have an instinct that enabled him to anticipate the gusts. Studying his technique Megan realised the lifeboat would not be following its present advantageous course without the young man's ability. They struggled on through the day with Rafferty doggedly bent over the tiller. It occurred to her that her earlier efforts when the wind had been blowing from astern had been a much easier way of sailing. She knew enough by now to accept that her sailing skills were extremely limited. She could see the fatigue beginning to take its toll of Rafferty and his concentration wavering a little. Desperately she prayed for a change in the wind, some abating, a shift to a more helpful direction perhaps; but the weather stayed constant. They talked about the conditions, agreeing that they were beyond Megan's newly acquired expertise. She broached the subject of rest but Rafferty shrugged off the suggestion. His determination impressed her but she knew in her heart of hearts that it was finite and once used up would leave the survivors in a parlous state. Some small part of her mind wished that David Watson were still with them.

Towards dawn on the eleventh day at sea since the loss of *Petrain Castle* the wind strength increased markedly, making the boat extremely difficult to control. Rafferty was forced to accept that to continue sailing was too dangerous and ordered the sail to be furled. He was no longer strong enough to stand up and was constrained, instead, to give his orders from his seat in the stern. Whether this fact contributed to the catastrophe that followed he would debate with himself for the rest of his life.

Two sailors stood to the mast. Bracing themselves against the boat's violent wave-induced movements, they released the halyard that held up the sail. The canvas immediately collapsed, its forward drive completely destroyed. Simultaneously its power to heel the clumsy vessel away from the wind was removed, but the majority of the survivors were seated to the windward side in an attempt to balance this power. The abruptly unbalanced lifeboat rolled viciously towards the wind and dipped its gunwale under the surface. Megan watched, frozen in her horror as bodies spilled overboard, caught unawares by the sudden motion. The two sailors at the mast who had unwittingly caused the disaster were flung into the sea yards from the craft. She saw a dark blob of a head briefly before it was overwhelmed by a wave. The boat continued to capsize until it was lying practically on its side in the disturbed water, the mast and sail pushed almost flat. At last there was some assistance from the wind as it held them from complete inversion; there was a balance—the boat was poised to roll over totally but the blasting air held it steady.

The stability was temporary and illusory. As men were thrust into the sea their instincts drove them to strike out for the surface. They drifted clear of the lifeboat. Megan found herself clinging to the tiller with one hand and the transom with the other as more men were washed away. Freed of the weight causing the capsize and assisted by the wind, the craft rolled back onto an even keel. There were no more than a handful of soaking figures left desperately clinging to the thwarts. Caught unawares, the majority of the survivors were now swimming for their lives. Megan glanced across at Rafferty who had mercifully survived also but who now seemed to be unable to react to the horrific situation. She instinctively knew that he had given all of his inner strength and would not be able to help further.

The boat continued to roll perilously in the waves and she could see that the wind was pushing them away from those in the water at an alarming rate. She cast around at her feet remembering some rope that had been there earlier. Her fingers closed around a thin heaving line. Without thinking of the dangers inherent in the act she stood and threw the end toward a cluster of bobbing heads. It fell well short.

"Damn!" she exclaimed in exasperation, realising that the bulk of the rope was still trapped under her feet. She tried again, this time with more success. The line fell close to an outstretched arm. A hand grasped it and pulled. Fortunately for Megan there was plenty of slack or she may well have been dragged into the bubbling sea as well. She braced herself to assist the swimmer's efforts and soon a head appeared at the gunwale. It was followed by an arm desperately seeking purchase to lever its owner aboard. She bent to tug at the limb and soon the muscular body of the Third Engineer lay panting in the bilges. As his strength returned he looked up at her and smiled gratefully.

Over the next half-hour they managed to save two more seamen: by then they were alone once more on the surface of the ocean. The nine who had survived this latest ordeal were exhausted and lay like dead things in the bottom of the lifeboat. Megan, still occupying her place at the stern, supported the limp frame of Dick Rafferty who had lapsed into unconsciousness. She dozed, moving freely to the unpredictable motion of the lifeboat as it pitched and tossed at the mercy of the weather. Events had gone beyond her. There was nothing further that could be done but she never stopped believing that she would survive.

CHAPTER 7

▼

The diminutive German sailor, Larsen, grinned at the four captives: "You go Germany!" Seeing their confusion, he continued in his broken English, "Ve meet *milch* cow. You go on."

"What on earth is he going on about?" queried David.

"I think he's talking about a supply submarine," replied Ellis. "I've heard the Germans have a number of big subs specially built to be able to transfer fuel and stores to the fighting boats."

UB-132 was on the surface and clearly proceeding at full speed, although until Larsen had spoken they had had no inkling as to why this was the case. The big diesels in the after part of the vessel were at full power and the whole structure shook and rattled under their influence. David assumed that it was dark although he had no means of confirming this, being incarcerated in the torpedo room. In fact, it was twilight and the U-boat commander was taking a slight risk of being spotted by aircraft in his efforts to make a rendezvous with his resupply vessel. He believed that, for the time being, his command was well away from the RAF's patrol routes and was therefore pressing on at maximum speed. For much of the voyage *UB-132* had been in areas off Africa where the RAF were unlikely to reach. Now, however, having come north, she was moving into a position where it was possible to be spotted by Coastal Command aircraft out of Gibraltar. The commander had been ordered to meet the supply submarine to replenish his diminished diesel fuel supplies. This would enable *UB-132* to remain on her patrol line for at least another month—a mixed blessing for the crew who had been looking forward to returning to their base in France for a spell of shore leave after an arduous but only moderately successful stint on patrol.

The U-boat ploughed on through the night rolling slightly in a relatively smooth sea. It was just after dawn that David was woken from a deep sleep by a change in the engine note. He sat up on the plank of wood that served as his bed, glancing across at his neighbour, Captain Ellis. Over on the other side of the space he could see one of the two Dutchmen also stirring.

"We must be at the rendezvous," muttered Ellis at the edge of wakefulness.

They listened as the engines slowed to a minor rumble before stopping altogether. There was still plenty of noise around them but the cessation of vibration came as a relief.

"What now, sir?"

"Your guess is as good as mine!" Unlike David Watson, Hubert Ellis was too long in the tooth to be particularly impatient.

They could hear orders being shouted in the control room and some of the sailors left the torpedo space. After almost an hour, Larsen appeared and beckoned to the four captives.

"Come! Come! You go now!"

He led them into the control room and indicated that they should scale the ladder at the base of the conning tower. The Dutchmen led the way followed by Captain Ellis with David bringing up the rear. He looked around the area gaining a confused impression of steel pipes and valves surrounding large control panels. There were some large chrome plated hand-wheels that he deduced, correctly, were used to direct the submarine when under the surface. A big circular gauge graduated in metres dominated one of the panels. He could also see a profusion of wires neatly clipped to metal trays and running above his head in a fore and aft direction. He became aware of the German sailors who were on watch staring at him curiously. Rather ordinary people on the whole, he thought as he set his foot on the steel rung of the ladder.

David emerged onto the deck of the U-boat to find it bathed in watery sunlight. A light breeze was blowing and he felt chilled after the moist warmth of the torpedo room. Captain Ellis nudged him pointing out over the starboard bow. Not more than a hundred yards away he could see another larger submarine wallowing in the swell.

Larsen, who was standing a little behind them, also pointed. "*Milch* cow!" he said.

Midway between the two U-boats was a small inflatable boat being energetically rowed toward them by a German sailor. As they watched, it bumped alongside and was secured in position with a painter. On board were a number of sacks that Watson assumed must be food; these were quickly hoisted aboard and then

Larsen was herding them toward the tiny craft. It was apparent that it could not accommodate all four captives at one time, so the two Dutchmen volunteered to lead. Ellis and Watson stood watching as the inflatable deposited its passengers on the larger submarine and returned.

"Looks like they've already taken fuel on board," said Ellis, nodding toward a small fresh oil stain on the casing just in front of the conning tower.

"She'll be off after more victims no doubt, then."

The inflatable was held alongside for them to embark and soon they were free of *UB-132*. At that moment David heard the distinct clanging of alarm bells coming from within their recent home. He glanced at the top of the conning tower just in time to see a white topped peaked cap disappearing from view. Within seconds the bow dipped beneath the surface of the sea as the U-boat surged ahead in a crash dive. With a flurry of disturbed water *UB-132* rapidly disappeared from view.

"That was a bit sudden, wasn't it!" exclaimed Ellis. "What the hell's going on?"

The German sailor had redoubled his efforts at the oars and the little inflatable was surging along magnificently. There were shouts from the supply submarine; then suddenly her decks cleared of seamen; steel hatches clanged shut and she began to follow her sister beneath the waves. Their German oarsman could hardly believe his eyes, simply staring with a shocked expression as his ship deserted him.

David became aware of a new sound. He looked up to see the most enormous aeroplane thundering towards them. It seemed to be aiming directly at them before it lifted slightly from its dive. It passed overhead when two bombs appeared from its giant shadow and plummeted into the confused water marking the recent position of the supply vessel. There were two loud yet muffled explosions accompanied by huge gouts of water; then the aircraft was to be seen banking hard around to make a second pass. David marvelled at the pilot's skill in dragging the huge machine back toward them so quickly. He could see now that it was a flying boat, a Sunderland, he suspected. Over the next few minutes the three men, with differing thoughts, witnessed four further attacks, but apart from a mass of confused water and a few dead fish, there appeared to be no successes. Eventually, with a slow waggle of its wings, the aircraft flew slowly away. They were left in their flimsy conveyance at the mercy of the waves.

An onlooker might have found an element of irony in the fact that both David Watson and Megan Baxendell together with the rest of the remaining survivors of the Petrain Castle sinking were all drifting in various parts of the Atlantic Ocean. That would have been to ignore the dangers of their respective situations.

The No.2 Lifeboat, now with a complement reduced to nine, drifted in bright morning sunlight, its occupants reviving and beginning to take stock of the situation. Dick Rafferty lay over the tiller, still unconscious and with Megan's arm locked around his shoulder lest he fall overboard. The Third Engineer who had identified himself as John Davies was sitting against the port side of the boat immediately behind two sailors. Further forward were Blake and Smith, the two Junior engineers, sharing a thwart. One of the greasers, Tom Edwards, was in the bow alongside Owen Carter, a stoker. Everyone was exhausted by the demands, both emotional and physical, of the past night. Megan realised this and decided that she must act swiftly to raise their spirits. Luckily the meagre food supplies and the water container had withstood the near capsize; she quickly organised a portion of milk tablets and biscuits washed down with a cup of water for each man. The meal was accepted thankfully by all bar one. A sailor slumped against the mast was found to have died in the night and it was with heavy hearts that they consigned his body to the sea. Somehow the death with its undeniable evidence was worse than the loss of people during the night.

"We should get the sail up again," stated Megan.

"But we can't sail this tub without the Third Mate," said John Davies doubtfully.

"The wind isn't that strong and it's from the south west; I should be able to handle her as things stand." Megan was far from confident but was concerned with morale. In her mind sailing would give everyone the feeling that progress was being made and might raise the spirits of those on board.

"I've got the course to steer. We must do something." She appealed to those in front of her.

For a moment she thought the men were going to ignore her, then one of the sailors stood, shuffled to the mast and heaved on the rope halyard. The lifeboat responded immediately to the pressure of the sail. A bubbly white moustache grew at the forefoot, rapidly extended along the side and was left behind in the confusion that was their wake. They were moving once again. Gently Megan disentangled Dick Rafferty's arm from the tiller; he mumbled something but did not wake as she laid him down on the seat. She pulled the tiller and swung the boat's head onto course. They sailed throughout the rest of the day making good mileage. The survivors began to develop some optimism; a regularly changed lookout system was established as they searched for the African coastline. It was agreed to drop the sail at nightfall if for no other reason than that Megan was exhausted after her efforts during the day.

They had no means of estimating drift due to any local currents so at daybreak the next day when they started off again Megan stuck to the same course. The activity associated with getting under way served to disturb Rafferty who slowly sat up blinking his eyes, his face carrying a slightly puzzled expression. Megan squinted at him thoughtfully, pleased to see that he looked altogether fitter with clear eyes and a less haggard countenance.

"Hi! Welcome back, how do you feel?" Megan couldn't resist putting a hand to his brow. He was significantly cooler she decided. Quickly putting him in the picture as to the events of the recent past she offered Rafferty the tiller.

"You seem to have done well enough without me," he smiled. "Carry on if you still feel up to it."

It was early evening when a shout from the bow made everyone sit up and stare forward expectantly.

"Land ahead!" The yell came from Stoker Carter.

Rafferty stood shading his eyes against the fading sunlight. He shook his head uncertainly. "Maybe, maybe not. We should be able to be more certain in a little while at the rate we're travelling."

The atmosphere in the lifeboat was transformed: there was hope and anticipation where before there had been depression and apathy. All eyes were focussed on the distant horizon, scanning the interface between the ocean and the sky expectantly. There was the faintest darkening away on the starboard bow. At first Rafferty thought it might be a rain squall rushing toward them; mentally he prepared to drop the sail and change course to meet it head on. Then it occurred to him that the smudge on the horizon scarcely appeared to be getting any closer. A squall would move quickly. He found himself hoping that this was at last the long hoped for landfall. As they sailed on the wind began to drop as if determined to keep them waiting as long as possible. Nightfall found them becalmed and still doubtful as to what they were seeing.

"We'll wait for the morning," said Rafferty. "Let's get the sail off her!"

"Do you think it is land?" asked John Davies.

Rafferty smiled but offered no opinion.

The night was a cool windless experience but for most on board there was little sleep: the prospect of setting foot on dry land once again was the source of their insomnia. The lifeboat rolled sluggishly and there was much discussion as to what the morrow would bring.

"Where do you think we are? I mean which country?" asked Megan.

"It hurts my professional pride but I have to admit I don't really know." Rafferty was clearly feeling much better and they chatted long into the night.

"What were you doing in Gibraltar?" he asked at one stage.

"Well actually I was nursing in the hospital there."

"Yes, I know that, Captain Ellis mentioned it." Rafferty persisted: "There are umpteen hospitals in Britain; why Gib of all places?"

"Oddly enough, although I didn't think about it at the time I guess I just wanted to get away and do something on my own. Daddy has always kept a close eye on me since Mum died. It was time I looked out for myself for a while; mind you, this war business showed that I wasn't really far from his influence." Megan grinned ruefully.

"Sorry about your mother," sympathised Rafferty.

"Um, some sort of problem with her blood; it hit Daddy hard, very hard indeed. I think that's why he tries to keep me close to him."

Megan smoothed her skirt over her knees and stared at her hands. The fingers were long, elegant even but looked red and swollen with the effects of sun and seawater. She realised she missed her father. Then came the acceptance that her present problems were ones she would have to solve without his help. She found that she didn't mind. She looked up at Rafferty. "So what about you? What brought you to a life at sea?"

"Nothing dramatic I'm afraid. My Dad is a captain on another of the Company's ships. Just followed in his footsteps I suppose."

It was apparent that the shy young Officer was not overly keen to talk about himself and the conversation gradually petered out. Megan found herself dozing but was jerked awake by a hand on her shoulder.

"I think we can get under way again." Rafferty pointed over the sea to where the first signs of the coming dawn were lightening the sky.

It took only minutes to raise the sail once more and continue their eastward progress. As the sun rose to issue in another day the survivors stared forward, seeking a glimpse of a landfall. There was none. The mood of hopeful anticipation began to drain away. By mid-morning a general gloom was beginning to envelop them; then, almost magically, a grey strip appeared on the horizon. In the brighter sunlight of the day there was, this time, little doubt that they had reached the coast. As the day wore on it became possible to pick out details, vegetation, a broad sandy beach and an extensive white-topped surf.

"I don't like the look of those waves," murmured Rafferty.

Megan turned toward him frowning uncertainly.

"It could capsize the boat," he offered by way of explanation.

CHAPTER 8

▼

It had been a long night. David had dozed off and on but genuine restful sleep had evaded him. God help us if the weather gets any worse, he thought as the encroaching dawn gradually painted the inflatable in sombre colours. A heavy swell, the aftermath of some distant storm possibly, had tormented them through the night though fortunately without too great a wind strength. The problem for the occupants of the tiny boat was a need to balance their craft as successive waves passed under them; on a number of occasions they had teetered on the brink of a capsize, only saved from being thrown into the heaving sea by a concerted shift of weight across the boat. Their dilemma had not been assisted by the language difficulty. Their German companion, still seated on the centre thwart he'd used as a rower, apparently spoke no English. He appeared friendly enough, despite the circumstances leading to their situation, but all communication was necessarily by sign language. The two Englishmen sat at either end of the inflatable but any attempt at conversation was inhibited by the bulk of the heavyset German seaman sitting between them.

Tired by the constant motion and the need to balance their craft, David was becoming increasingly worried by the size of the approaching seas. It wasn't that they were getting larger, rather that they were not decreasing. He doubted that the weary three men could continue to control their vessel for very much longer. He looked at Captain Ellis, slumped at the stern and looking exhausted, thinking that the old man would not be much further help as the day wore on.

"What do you think of our chances, sir!" he shouted at the recumbent form.

"Eh, what?" came the startled response.

"I was wondering whether or not the subs might come back for us?"

"Umm, your guess is as good as mine." Ellis was in no mood for talking and the dialogue lapsed.

The morning dragged on without further disaster although there were a few close calls, as on occasion they lay suspended on the face of a wave with the inflatable suspended at a crazy angle approaching the vertical. On each occasion they managed to save the situation, just. Luckily, Fritz, as David had unoriginally christened the German sailor, was showing less signs of fatigue than the others and was clearly fully aware of the threat the disturbed sea represented. David developed the habit of scanning the surrounding ocean as they crested a wave but there was nothing to be seen. Then towards the middle of the afternoon he saw it, indeed he almost missed the tiny speck, so used had he become to the barrenness of the surrounding seascape.

"There's an aircraft!" he yelled excitedly. "Look over to starboard...see it...just above the horizon!" Ellis and Fritz gazed in the direction of his outstretched arm, their mild interest suddenly transformed into wholehearted enthusiasm as they too spotted the moving spot. The silhouette gradually enlarged and hardened into the identifiable shape of a flying boat as it swept toward them.

"Looks like a Sunderland!" shouted Ellis. "Let's hope he sees us."

The huge four-engined machine maintained its course and passed within a mile of the inflatable but gave no indication of having seen them. David felt the bubble of excitement collapse in his chest; he couldn't believe it. Surely they had been spotted! He'd seen the pilots outlined in the windows of their cockpit; they, in their turn, couldn't have avoided seeing the survivors!

The Sunderland dwindled into nothingness in the brightness of the afternoon sky. They were alone once more. To David it seemed twice as lonely now after the brief moment of excitement.

"Cheer up, lad," grunted Ellis, seeing David's crestfallen expression, "If they're on patrol out of Gibraltar they could be back."

David smiled weakly, not really believing the older man but grateful for the encouraging words. Somehow grasping the feelings of the young Englishman without understanding the words, Fritz turned and patted David on the knee in a strangely reassuring gesture.

As it happened, the Sunderland never did return, but what did appear was the slim grey shape of a Royal Navy frigate. It steamed purposefully toward their position; then, as they watched, rounded up onto a course parallel to their line of drift and stopped. A boat was lowered and was soon alongside.

"Come on me lads, let's be having yer!" yelled a burly petty officer as he threw a light heaving line across to the inflatable.

When he reached the safety of the rescue craft David found himself wondering whether Megan had also been picked up by friendly forces.

Lifeboat No2 was in fact in sight of safety, yet separated from an inviting beach by crashing surf.

"I think we should follow the coast line south, see if we can find a safer landing place!" shouted Rafferty to those in the boat. "The risk of that lot turning the boat over is too great," he said quietly to Megan with a nod toward the surf line.

With a quick couple of orders and a skilful movement of the rudder, Rafferty gybed the vessel onto a course parallel to the shore. There was a small headland ahead but they continued in the same direction, thereby coming closer to the surf. From their seaward position it was difficult to judge the height of the waves smashing into the beach: they could only judge the ferocity of the ocean from the thunderous noise of its breaking on the golden sand.

"I reckon we could do it, Three-Oh," came a voice from the bow.

There were other voices raised in agreement but Rafferty ignored them. He was a better judge of the conditions and considered the risks to be too great. He did not however take into account the impetus lent to men who had suffered the privations of days afloat in an under provisioned lifeboat and who were now looking at apparent salvation being bypassed.

Suddenly a sailor sitting in front of the Third Engineer stood up.

"I'm going to try," he yelled as he stood on the gunwale and plunged into the azure sea. Gripped by the same enthusiasm his mate followed immediately and soon Megan could see two dark heads moving toward the beach swimming strongly.

Rafferty shook his head sadly. "I wish they'd stayed with us, the undertow…" He left the sentence hanging in the air like some unsought judgement. They all stared after the swimmers as they headed slowly shoreward. There was about fifty yards to cover in relatively smooth water before they would be in the surf line. The lifeboat sailed on, leaving the sailors astern.

"We should go back," said Megan voicing the thoughts of the majority.

Rafferty nodded and soon they were following a reciprocal course. The swimmers were into the first of the breaking waves, still moving strongly. A huge breaker obscured them for a moment but then the two heads reappeared, one still facing the beach, the other looking seaward and apparently stationary. The second figure was in trouble, it was clear, but his companion was continuing shoreward unawares. Megan had her hand to her mouth as the struggling swimmer was overwhelmed by another wave. He disappeared again, then amazingly his head came up and he was to be seen being carried by the wave into the beach. What happened next was not clear to the seaward observers; undoubtedly the visible specks of humanity reached the beach either by their own efforts or by the strength of the waves. They saw two heads at the water's edge one instant; the next they had gone, plucked back by the implacable might of the sea. Rafferty sailed backwards and forwards parallel to the beach as everyone strained their eyes searching for the men. It was a wasted effort: the sailors had vanished.

There was a gloomy silence in the lifeboat as Rafferty brought them round again onto a southerly course: there was nothing that could be done for the two seamen. They sailed on slowing as the wind lightened. The coastline did not appear to become any more inviting as they progressed.

"If we don't find somewhere soon we'll have to get the oars out again," observed Rafferty.

"We won't have to spend another night out here, will we?" asked John Davies.

Rafferty shrugged non-committally. At that moment any doubts about a landing were abruptly resolved as the lifeboat crashed into a rogue spur of rock lurking just a foot or two below the surface. Two planks near the bow were shattered and water began to pour in. The bowmen shuffled sternwards in an attempt to lift the damaged area clear of the sea's surface, but it was impossible. Ominously the craft began to settle.

"Drop the sail! Get the oars shipped!" Rafferty's shouted order galvanised the crew. "Quickly, we've got to turn her!"

It was the work of just minutes to get the heavy oars from their stowage position and into their rowlocks but in that time the boat had been carried a long way, broadside, by the swell. They were now much closer to the shore.

"Pull hard, starboard," yelled Rafferty, his voice shrill with concern. "Back up, port."

The cumbersome boat gradually pivoted under the influence of the straining oarsmen.

"Hold it," Rafferty twitched the rudder as the stern rose to an incoming wave. "Got it!" he exclaimed, as the boat's bow remained facing toward the beach as the sea forced them forward. "Hold her stern to the waves," he encouraged the rowers. "We mustn't allow her to come broadside again or we'll be rolled over."

The next wave was safely negotiated. The thrash of breakers on the beach was now a continuous roar coming closer every second. Megan was appalled by the mass of white spray obscuring all but the smallest glimpse of the shore above the timeline. Another wave passed safely.

"When we hit, everyone get ashore by the bow as quickly as possible and get clear of the water!" shouted Rafferty.

The lifeboat was nearly half full now and the rowers were having increasing difficulty following his orders. Yet somehow the stern kept lifting to successive waves without the boat broaching.

"Get ready, next wave should do it!"

A particularly fearsome comber reared up behind them but this time, instead of passing under them, it began to break as it reached them. There was nothing more Rafferty could do. He stared in fascination at the monster. The wave simultaneously lifted their stern somewhat and then filled it with water. Megan was drenched, gasping for breath. Suddenly there was a heart-stopping bang from forward followed by a rasping, grating sound as the heavy boat was thrust up the beach. It stopped moving and Megan began to heave a sigh of relief only to find her arm being pulled.

"Come on, we've got to get off before the sea smashes this lot to bits."

Rafferty was pulling her to her feet; she followed obediently, still not really sure in her mind what was happening. Her confusion remained as she stepped over thwarts, up to the bow then half jumped half fell on to the wet sand. Rafferty joined her and dragged her up the beach to where the rest of the survivors had congregated. They flopped down in hot soft golden sand and watched a wave smash into their erstwhile conveyance; within minutes it was reduced to matchwood and carried away by the undertow.

"Well done, Three-Oh," said an anonymous voice quietly. There was an agreeing rumble from the others as the shock of their narrow escape began to hit the group. Now just seven in number, the tiny band lay a long time on the burning beach recovering. Rafferty had driven himself to the limit and found it difficult to motivate his fellow castaways; it was the engineer John Davies who eventually stood and said, "We should try to find out where we are before nightfall, lads." One by one the tired bodies were levered upright and they began to plod up the beach.

CHAPTER 9

▼

It felt strange to be back on dry land, particularly in England. David Watson was new to Liverpool but he felt no interest in exploring the city. Ever since he had learned where the ship he was on was due to discharge its cargo he had determined to head straight home to the Clyde on arrival. He left the Albert dock and headed for Lime Street railway station. He carried no baggage—that had all disappeared with Petrain Castle; indeed, he was indebted to the Captain of Elysian for the gift of the warm wool jacket he was wearing. The garment was a more appropriate replacement for the uniform coat he had inadvertently received from the Chief Engineer of the sunken vessel.

After the fortuitous rescue by the Royal Navy he had been transferred to the cargo ship, *Elysian*, to augment an engineering department that had been woefully short staffed due to illness and the effects of the war. Captain Ellis had remained with Fritz aboard the frigate; the former suffering somewhat from the effects of exposure from his sojourn in the inflatable boat, the latter for security reasons. David had wished them both well when the warship's doctor had declared him fit and he had been transferred to the merchantman. He felt a bond with them as a result of their shared experiences and he experienced a brief moment of sadness at the parting. It did not seem odd to him to include the German in his feelings: the man was after all as far as David was concerned just another shipmate.

At the railway station he looked up the times of trains. There was no direct connection for Glasgow that day but he found his eye drawn to a departure time for London. If he ran he might just catch that train; without stopping to think about it he sprinted impulsively to the ticket office, bought a single and within minutes found himself southbound on the express. It was with a feeling of surprise that he took stock of the situation as he stood in the overcrowded corridor. He had no defined intention for any visit to the capital and precious little money with which to enjoy any stay. Perhaps, he mused, he could draw his back pay from the main offices of the owners of *Petrain Castle*.

The train rattled on through the afternoon occasionally stopping though for what reason David was at first unsure. Then, above the rattle and crash of the carriage as it sped along the rails, he heard a new sound. A thunderous roar moved from one side of his perception to the other as a large twin-engined aircraft swooped over the train. He stared at it, shocked to see the black crosses on the wings and fuselage. It dawned upon him that this was the enemy, a threat to his well-being. Luckily the raider did not attack but continued on its low-level cross-country course.

"One of they Junkers 88's, I reckon," averred a scrawny individual looking untidy in an overlarge Royal Navy ratings uniform.

Watson glanced worriedly at the sailor lounging behind him. "Does this happen often?"

The man laughed. "Where the 'ell 'ave you been, laddie? There's a war on you know!"

He stared at David for a moment, his face taking on a more serious expression.

"'ow comes a big strong lad like you is still in civvies, eh?"

David reacted guiltily to the suspicious rating. "Oh, I'm an engineer at sea."

The man continued to stare.

"Merchant Navy…my ship was sunk."

His words were rewarded with a broad grin and an outstretched hand. David shook it gratefully mumbling his name.

"Fred Gates, pleased to meet ye."

The train was now only minutes short of its destination at Euston but with a heavy clanking of compressing buffers it stopped abruptly. It remained there for an hour whilst an air raid was in progress over the capital. Gates proved to be talkative at least about the progress of the war. His descriptions of the various recent reverses as the German war machine spread across mainland Europe left David feeling gloomy. The conversation shifted to David's experiences and he found himself chatting freely about the loss of *Petrain Castle* and the subsequent sequence of events. He didn't mention Megan but in his mind's eye he had a clear picture of her sitting in the lifeboat as he was hustled aboard the U-boat.

Somewhere in the distance a siren wailed.

"Thank goodness for that…the All Clear. Jerry must 'ave gone 'ome."

Fred Gates looked pleased. "We'll be on our way again in a mo'!"

Sure enough, within minutes the train clanked back into motion and they recommenced their journey.

"Where you staying?" asked the soldier as they approached the platform at Euston.

"Er, well I'm not sure just yet. Might try somewhere down the docks."

Gates sucked his teeth dramatically at the same time shaking his head firmly. "No, no, no you don't want to be going there. That's where Jerry keeps on unloading his bombs." He regarded David critically, his head at a slight angle. "Look, lad, I'm on forty eight 'ours leave. You could doss down wi' me at me mother's if you wanted. 'Ave me brother's bed. 'E's in the army, somewhere."

There seemed little way that David could refuse the offer graciously so he accepted. It resolved his immediate problem and, truth to tell, he had warmed to the little Cockney sailor.

Mrs. Gates turned out to be a plump warm lady with a twinkle in her eye. She took to Watson immediately, making him feel at home in her little terraced house. There did not appear to be a Mr. Gates senior and David did not raise the matter. The home was scrupulously clean with a cherished albeit well worn feel about it.

"Sit yourself down," invited Mrs. Gates. "We'll have a cup of tea."

Later that evening after a filling if unadventurous meal, which Mrs. Gates apologised for, blaming "the War", David and Fred fell to yarning about the sea. Much of their conversation proved anecdotal as they admitted to each other that they had each only spent a minimal time actually at sea. Fred explained that he was a "Hostilities Only" rating, recruited along with many others to fill the gaps in a Royal Navy stretched dangerously thin by the exigencies of war. It transpired that he had been trained as a Seaman Gunner and was on leave before joining a merchant ship that was presently being armed for convoy duty. For some reason the name of the ship was not mentioned until the two young men were tidying up before retiring.

"What did you say the name of your ship was?" asked David.

"Er, 'ang on, I can't remember exactly…something *Castle* I think. It's on me travel warrant,"

"*Castle*?" repeated David, his interest rising.

"Yeah, there it is," Fred brandished a slightly dog-eared scrap of paper. "It sez 'ere *Arthurian Castle*, Port Glasgow."

"Good Lord, that's one of the ships of the Line I worked for: *Petrain* was a later addition to the fleet." David beamed at his friend, digesting the coincidence.

Gates' small skinny face cracked into a grin. "Garn! You mean we're nearly shipmates!"

David laughed out loud at the wisecrack. "Well only 'nearly'—but seriously, she's a good ship; you'll be all right there."

When he awoke the next morning after a good night's sleep David Watson found himself thinking about Fred and *Arthurian Castle*. He lay there looking at the early morning sunlight seeping in through cracks in the blackout curtaining which he had neglected to secure properly. He came to a decision as the bedroom door vibrated to a light tapping.

"Are you awake and decent?" came Mrs. Gates' voice as, without waiting for a reply, she swept into the room. "Thought you might like a cuppa. Breakfast's in ten minutes." Like a windjammer under full sail she left him and he heard her slippers clacking on the stairs as she returned to the kitchen.

The meal turned out to be scrambled egg on toast preceded by a bowl of porridge.

"Sorry we've no bacon and the egg's powdered," explained Mrs. Gates.

David had to admit the taste was somewhat unusual but he was hungry enough to eat almost anything and he wolfed it down quickly.

"Where's Fred? Not up, yet?"

"Good gracious, he was away out almost an hour ago! Said he'd see you later. He's after seeing some of his old mates I shouldn't wonder. You might catch him in the Weaver's Arms around the middle of the day." She explained where the pub was situated before busying herself brewing another cup of tea.

But David had ideas of his own for the day. He thanked Mrs. Gates for the breakfast, consulted her briefly about public transport and soon left the house on his quest. It was late morning before he stepped off the open-topped double-decker bus and walked the short distance into St Mary Axe. It was a short rather narrow street in the City of London filled with a number of imposing buildings. He wandered down the pavement searching. It was near the end that he saw something he recognised; it was a flag, a similar one in fact to that which had flown so proudly from the masthead of *Petrain Castle* when she was delivered to her Owners. He stopped under the flag and looked at the building's façade. So this is Head Office, he thought as he walked up a short flight of stairs past two open ornate iron gates into a large open space. He stood still momentarily overwhelmed by the sheer size. There was a small desk to one side with an elderly uniformed man watching him closely. He marched across the marbled floor and presented himself to the official.

"I'm David Watson—I'd like to see Mr. Baxendell, please." He spoke quickly, his voice squeaky with nerves.

The man laughed out loud, "Do you now?"

David scowled. "Yes. He *is* here, isn't he?"

"Oh, he's here all right, but why would a young lad like you be wanting to talk to Sir William?"

"I was on *Petrain Castle.*"

A pair of sharp eyes regarded him speculatively for a moment. "And what about her?"

"She was sunk off Africa by a German submarine."

The man's face twitched into an expression of surprise mingled with a touch of respect.

"Wait here," he commanded after a moment's thought.

The commissionaire disappeared to return within minutes with a middle-aged bespectacled woman.

"You were on *Petrain*?" she asked without preamble.

David nodded.

"Come with me."

He was led up a wide stone staircase, through a door into a small heavily carpeted office.

"Stay here a moment, I'll see if he's free."

She slipped through a side door, then reappeared beckoning him to join her. He stepped past her into a large wood panelled room. To one side two huge picture windows looked out onto the street. A substantial bookcase occupied another wall but it was the man behind the desk immediately in front of him that captured David's attention. To say that he was imposing would have been misleading; even seated behind the desk he appeared of only medium height with grey thinning hair, but David was impressed nonetheless. There was an air of power, of determination about the man that could not be denied.

"Please take a seat. Can Miss Sharp get you a drink? Tea? Coffee?"

David shook his head as he eased himself onto a chair, trying not to be overawed by the situation.

Sir William dismissed his secretary who had been hovering by the interconnecting door, then regarded him levelly, weighing him up. "If you were on our ship how come I didn't hear of your survival?"

"Well, sir, Captain Ellis and I were picked up more by luck than anything by a frigate escorting a convoy northward from Gibraltar. We docked in Liverpool yesterday. I'm sure the skipper will be in contact fairly soon; he stayed on the frigate which was continuing on to the Clyde with the rest of the convoy."

David explained the circumstances of the loss of the ship, the mistaken identity that saw him taken aboard the U-boat and gave brief details of the rescue from the drifting inflatable.

Sir William interrupted only occasionally with the odd question of clarification. At the end of the account he sat back in his seat.

"Did you know my daughter was on board?"

"Yes sir, we all did. Joined in Gib. I was with her after we were torpedoed." Suddenly David realised the reason for the impulse that had brought him to London: he was seeking news of Megan! Forgetting for a moment where he was he blurted out, "Is there any news of the lifeboats of Megan, er, I mean Miss Baxendell, sir?"

His interviewer smiled briefly at the outburst. "No, lad, yours is the first news of the ship since she left port, hence my interest. Damn the Navy for not radioing in that they had picked up survivors! Now that I know that she's alive, er, that there are more survivors, I can make enquiries through our West African agents. Tell me, was my daughter fit and well? Not injured in the shelling?"

For an instant David glimpsed the worried parent through Sir William's businessman's veneer and felt a flush of sympathy for the older man.

"I helped her into the lifeboat myself. She was fine. They should have reached land by now. I'm an engineer, not a navigator, but Captain Ellis seemed to think they had a damned good chance of getting ashore in one piece."

"Thank you for that," said Baxendell, standing up and proffering his hand. "I'm afraid you must excuse me now. I'm late already for a meeting."

David shook the hand and turned to leave; as he reached the door the man spoke again.

"If there's anything I can do for you, please ask."

It was then that Watson remembered his decision of that morning as he lay in bed. "Well, sir, as a matter of fact there is." He paused, watching the baronet who nodded.

"I'd like to sail on your ship *Arthurian Castle*, if its possible, sir."

"Possible? You obviously don't know how scarce experienced Merchant Navy engineers are with this war on. I'll be more than happy to arrange it although why you should forego your survivor's leave entitlement I don't understand. You do know she's sailing very shortly, don't you?"

David nodded sharply, mildly amused by the baronet's rapid switch from concerned father back to efficient businessman.

"Here's what you do: report to our Glasgow office and they will fix you up. I'll send them a note."

David left the offices in a state of bewilderment at the turn of events. He was employed again with back wages in his pocket and even a travel voucher to get him home to the Clyde, courtesy of the helpful Miss Sharp. He'd even shaken hands with his employer, an unthinkable event at the time of the launch of *Petrain Castle*. Life felt good as he retraced his earlier steps along St. Mary Axe. It was a pity that there had been no news of Megan but somehow that did not worry him. That there would be good news in the future he was certain.

When he returned to the Gates' house it was to find Fred in an easy chair sleeping off the effects of his visit to the Weaver's Arms. Mrs. Gates held a finger to her lips and ushered David into the kitchen. Over the inevitable pot of tea they talked about the Blitz, the period of 56 days in 1940 when the German Luftwaffe tried to break the spirit of a nation by pounding London with bombs and land-mines. David had seen something of the devastation caused in his journey to the City. Great gaps had been torn in rows of houses, the wonder being why some buildings had survived when their neighbours had been reduced to rubble. Even in the City offices had been demolished although Mrs. Gates maintained that the East End of London and the dockland areas had borne the brunt of the attacks. She related tales of sleeping on the platforms of the Elephant and Castle Underground station at the height of the onslaught. Fortunately her house and street had survived the bombing. The Luftwaffe still flew over Britain but in smaller numbers and to different targets. London had survived and, more importantly, so had the morale of the people.

"We still get the odd raid but that's all," she was saying as Fred sleepily wandered into the kitchen.

"Got a cuppa on the go, Mum?"

Fred sat drinking the tea as his senses attuned fully to wakefulness; eventually he turned to David.

"And where 'ave you been this bright and sunny day?"

David gave him an edited version of his experiences in the Shipping Company offices. He mentioned his back pay and the need to find another seagoing berth but made no reference to Megan or her father. He preferred to keep memories of the young lady to himself.

"Actually," he concluded, "it looks as though I might be on your ship."

"What, never!" Fred was clearly both surprised and pleased, "I don't believe it!"

"I'll need to check in with the Glasgow office when I get home, but anyway I'll travel up with you tomorrow."

"Well, I'll eat my hat! That's great. What do you think, Mum?"

Mrs. Gates smiled happily. "I think it's time I was getting some dinner into you two."

They managed to get aboard a directly routed train the following evening. It was officially a sleeper but all the designated compartments were fully booked, not that they could have afforded one. David and Fred could not find a seat in the overfilled carriages and had to settle for a corner of a packed corridor where it was just possible for them to sit. The journey was long and tedious with numerous stops and delays of varying lengths. David came to accept this as being a normal part of travelling in wartime Britain. He dozed in a hunched position propped up against his pal. They were both very relieved when their journey was finally over and they emerged onto the platform of Glasgow's Waverly station, dishevelled and travel-worn.

"I guess we have to split up now," said David after they had passed through the ticket barrier.

"Yeah, the Navy'll 'ave me if I don't report in as soon as possible. 'Ope to see you on board then?"

David smiled, nodding firmly. "I'll see the Owner's superintendent when the office opens."

Fred hoisted his kitbag onto his shoulder, waved and strode off, soon to be swallowed up by the throng of departing passengers.

C H A P T E R   10

▼

So this is going to be my home for the foreseeable future, thought David Watson, staring around the stark cubicle of his cabin. It comprised a bunk to one side, a settee to another and a stainless steel wash-hand basin just inside the doorway. A small wardrobe alongside a tiny desk section completed the furnishings. The woodwork was dark and stained in places, lending a gloomy appearance to a space illuminated naturally by a single porthole.

Arthurian Castle was an older vessel than his previous ship and did not compare particularly favourably. She was similar in layout although built on the Tyne by John Redhead & Sons in 1932. Surprisingly, the main propulsion engine was virtually the same, a factor that had presumably influenced the local superintendent's decision to promote him to Fourth Engineer. David was proud of his advancement if a little nervous about taking up his more responsible duties. His new Chief Engineer, a Yorkshireman with the unlikely name of Fraser McKay, was a hearty friendly bull of a man who had welcomed David aboard with a vigorous handshake. There had been an instant respect between the two men that boded well for the upcoming voyage.

The ship was berthed in Port Glasgow discharging a general cargo and David had joined her as the last few items were being winched ashore. He'd had a day at home after visiting the Shipping Line's offices. True to his promise, Sir William Baxendell had advised the superintendent of David's wish to join *Arthurian Castle* and it was a matter of only a few minutes to complete the formalities of signing Articles. It was made clear that David had accrued leave from his time aboard *Petrain Castle* and the official shook his head when David stated his preference to forgo his entitlement.

He enjoyed his day at home regaling his parents with details of the torpedoing and his incarceration aboard the U-boat. Somehow he contrived to make the events sound like an adventure almost free of risk. His father was clearly proud of him, insisting on taking his son to the local where the stories could be reiterated over copious amounts of watery beer. Disappointment clouded his mother's face when he explained that he was joining another ship the following day.

"I want to stay with the same ship owner if possible...the chance came up so I took it. Besides, I know one of the lads on board," he tried to justify himself to the unhappy woman.

She was not to be mollified. "Tommy Waddington will be annoyed he missed ye. He's talking about shipping out but the Yard are saying he can't go. Anyway, what about Eileen McFee—she always asks after ye when I see her?"

David had no real reply to offer so he stood up and gave her a big hug instead. Truth to tell he wasn't sure why he'd opted for *Arthurian Castle* rather than some leave and then whatever ship came along. Certainly Fred Gates would be a good shipmate but that was scarcely reason enough. It did occur to him, though, that being on a *Castle* ship might enable him to glean information regarding Megan's well-being.

Once the last of the imported cargo had been discharged they received orders to shift to another berth where a new cargo would be available. The move was not unexpected but the sacks and boxes that were loaded into the capacious holds caused something of a stir on board. No new destination had been announced in accordance with Wartime regulations and it was normal for ship's crews to speculate on their discharge port based on the cargo they loaded. The initial 2000 tons of flour in sacks, which was stowed in No 3 Hold, was accepted without comment and even the coal which went in the aftermost Hold didn't seem too far from the ordinary. It was the drums of aviation petrol secured at the bottom of No 1 Hold that got the rumourmongers working overtime. The medical supplies and small quantities of cigarettes, spirits and biscuits only added to the debate as to where they were headed.

Eventually, her holds filled and battened down for the voyage, *Arthurian Castle* moved out to anchor in the Clyde at the Tail of the Bank. They stayed there two days before moving again, this time to Bowling a little closer to Glasgow where they were fitted with anti-aircraft armament. This comprised mainly 20 mm Oerlikon guns although they did receive one Bofors 40 mm in addition. At the last minute a couple of small Hotchkiss's were installed, one at each end of the bridge. An existing 4-inch gun at the stern was thoroughly overhauled and passed as fully operational by the Naval Officer supervising this work.

It was during this period that David renewed his acquaintance with Fred Gates. This worthy was to be in charge of the Low Angle 4-inch party and he spent much of the time alongside at Bowling ensuring that the gun's ammunition was safely stowed.

"So where are we going then?" asked Fred one evening after a busy day.

"I thought you would be able to tell me," replied David.

"Nah, their Lordships of the Admiralty ain't took me into their confidence jus' yet," grinned the Cockney. "Mind you wi' all these guns it can't be a milk run they've got in mind!"

They stood chatting at the ship's rail, debating the likelihood of various ports being their ultimate destination until it was time for David to go on watch in the engineroom. If they had known where *Arthurian Castle* was headed they might have enjoyed their last night in port rather less.

Heading down the Clyde once again David Watson remembered an earlier occasion when he had sailed this way: the sea trials of *Petrain Castle* seemed a lifetime away as he stood in front of the engine controls ready for any telegraph command from the bridge. This time he was in charge of the watch and responsible for all the engineroom machinery whilst on duty. He recalled the large number of shipyard fitters who had been present on the trials and smiled as he contrasted those men with his three assistants he now had. The oil-fired steam boilers were tended in the stokehold by a single fireman. In the main engine room there was another engineer and a greaser whose job it was to keep the massive bearings of the reciprocating engine fully supplied with oil.

They were steaming at Half Ahead with the Pilot still on board on their way to join a convoy being assembled in the Bristol Channel. Some vessels had already left the Clyde to join it and *Arthurian Castle* was hastening to catch them up. The big brass telegraph clanked, its bell ringing as the pointer shifted to Full Ahead. David acknowledged the order and spun the big horizontal control wheel of the main steam valve. Gradually the engine accelerated and the din in the engineroom increased significantly. He watched the mechanical revolution indicator steady on 74 rpm and stepped back from the controls, satisfied. His eyes roamed the engine space checking gauges; everything seemed to be fine and he relaxed slightly. The beginning of a new voyage was always a more worrying time, as machinery left idle for a period was once again required to operate correctly.

They reached the Pilot station and stopped briefly for him to leave. Under way once more, it was a simple matter of gradually bringing the main engine up to its full power and firing the boilers to match. Once set, David knew, the plant would require little adjustment through the rest of his watch. In harness with his assistants he therefore took particular care in his work.

Just short of midnight the Third Engineer and his team arrived to take over the watch.

"How's everything, Wattie?" asked the Third using a nickname which had appeared soon after David joined the ship.

"Nothing to worry about, really. The feed pump seems to be a bit noisy but I can't see anything wrong."

After a few further words David left the engineroom, took a quick shower and retired to his bunk to read a book he'd found left by a previous occupant of the cabin. He was pleased with the way his first seagoing watch had gone; he felt tired but quietly satisfied as his eyes closed and he drifted off into a deep sleep.

During the next few days life aboard *Arthurian Castle* settled into the inevitable regular routine. David stood his watches, took his meals and slept: in between times there was the opportunity for the odd game of cards with other off duty engineers and he often yarned with his friend, the gunner Fred Gates. It was during one of these chats that the subject of their ultimate destination came up once more. The ship was still a hotbed of rumour as no official announcement had yet been made although thoughts had now been more sharply focussed as they forged their way southwards. The other members of the convoy had emerged from mist as they approached the mouth of the Bristol Channel and the whole group had been shuffled into their required positions under the close attentions of the Royal Navy escorts.

"So what's the latest buzz? Where are we going?" David knew Gates to be close to the source of most rumours.

For once his friend seemed less than his normal ebullient self. "You're not gonna believe what I heard today," he began.

"Well?" prompted David impatiently as his companion hesitated.

"Well, you might ask…seems one of the AB's reckons the medical crates were stencilled with 'Malta' as the port of discharge."

David looked stunned, "Malta," he repeated almost to himself. It was well known that that little island was struggling to survive, having been all but isolated by the combined might of the German and Italian forces, both naval and airborne. The gallant inhabitants, civilians and British forces alike, were gradually being starved into submission by an enemy bent on preserving its supply lines to North Africa. There was absolutely no doubt that Malta at that time of the war held an enormous tactical significance for each side. Supplies to the island had been limited to that which could be carried in large submarines and fast minelayers. Due to the power of the Axis forces, sending merchant ships through the Mediterranean was an expensive and extremely hazardous undertaking requiring a huge escort presence. The thought of being sent there was a sobering one for the two friends sitting in a cabin aboard *Arthurian Castle*.

"Maybe we'll just drop them off at Gibraltar and then continue south around the Cape," suggested David.

"'Ave you looked at all them escorts out there? Seems 'eck of a lot to me for an 'andful of cargo ships," Gates replied wryly. "We've even got an aircraft carrier."

David was still loath to accept the idea. "Surely it's too dangerous for us; hell, we've only got a handful of pop-guns to defend ourselves with. Besides, it's the Navy's job to fight the enemy, not ours!"

"And we'll do our best," rapped Fred with pride.

"Sorry, mate, I wasn't getting at you!"

"Yeah, I know. Anyway, what really got to me was the stencilling."

"I don't follow?" David looked puzzled.

"See if the crates is in the sheds telling everyone where they'se going to it wouldn't take much for a German spy to find out!"

David's face was a picture as, with the dawning of understanding, his expression changed from one of puzzlement to disbelief and then concern.

Fred could not help grinning for an instant at the display but then his sombre mood returned. "We'll be sitting ducks with every Jerry an' Eyetie jus' ready an' waiting. Bit of incompetence somewhere is going to make life a bit interesting shortly, eh?"

The next afternoon after his watch David spent some time on deck examining the Naval fleet deployed around them. He had to admit there were an awful lot of them; perhaps more importantly, he caught a glimpse in the hazy sunlight of a series of capital ships. Battleships and aircraft carriers, he thought, this has to be serious, very serious.

The convoy entered the straits between Gibraltar and the North African coast and then deployed into its proper formation. The escorts had topped up with fuel oil either from the attendant fleet oilers or by diverting into the fuelling berths at the Rock. There could be no doubt now as to their destination and the masters of the cargo vessels were allowed to open sealed orders that confirmed the fact. The knowledge was passed on to their respective crews where it was received with general stoicism but a fair amount of discussion. The stage was now set for Operation Pedestal. Fourteen merchant ships protected by two battleships, three aircraft carriers and seven cruisers together with their destroyer screen entered the Mediterranean Sea braced for a brutal confrontation with massed enemy forces.

The convoy speed had been set at fifteen knots and David Watson for one knew that *Arthurian Castle* would be hard pressed to maintain that rate of advance for an extended period. The worst thing was that if they ever fell astern of the convoy there would be only a minimal prospect of the ship regaining her position, so little reserve of speed did she have.

As it happened, the freighter's capabilities were sorely tried the first night into the Mediterranean. It was normal for the burners used to spray fuel into the furnaces of the boilers to be changed for cleaning at the beginning of each watch. In a practised movement the firemen would shut off the fuel to a particular burner, release it, slip the cleaned replacement into place and reconnect the fuel supply. Under high pressure the fuel would spray in whirling mist and re-ignite from the heat retained in the furnace. On that particular evening the routine was followed normally but almost immediately it was reported to the engineer of the watch who happened to be Watson that there was a fire in the centre boiler. For an instant David thought he was having his leg pulled; after all, it was to be expected that the boiler was being fired, but the wide eyed, frightened face of the fireman told him otherwise. He brushed past the man and dashed into the stokehold. He could see the boilers apparently firing normally but then he noticed a telltale dull red glow coming from the steel plates forming the centre boiler windbox. He leapt across the space feeling the heat radiating from the air supply trunking and wrestled with the fuel shut off valve. For an instant it resisted his efforts to operate, his hands slick with sweat slipping on the painted handwheel, then it began to turn. Soon it was closed. The fires in the three individual furnaces died and went out, leaving a muted glow visible through the mica observation ports.

He stood back, momentarily satisfied, then to his horror realised that the fire was still raging unchecked in the windbox. The shock threw his mind into another gear; time seemed to dilate as he wrestled with the problem. Clearly fuel had entered the air supply plenum and was burning freely. His interruption of the fuel supply was only half a solution: within minutes the thin steel plate would melt and the flames would spill into the boiler-room. That could spell disaster in an area greasy with the fuel residues inevitable in such a space despite assiduous cleaning by the firemen. He had to get at the seat of the fire and attack it with an extinguisher, he reasoned. Fortunately the design of the front of the boiler allowed for the burners to be mounted on large, hinged plates which could be opened for cleaning. David seized a steel bar used for clearing furnace clinker and thumped the retaining clips. A quick levering and the plate swung back, revealing a huge ball of flame like something out of Dante's Inferno. He ducked back instinctively, his eyebrows singing in the blast of released heat. The fireman was at his elbow pulling a large red painted cylinder behind him. The two small wheels of its support bumped across the steel plates as he manhandled the large fire extinguisher into place.

It was the sort that produced foam when laid horizontal. David grabbed the device tugging it over to land with a crash on the plates. He grasped the rubber tube with its shut off cock and directed it at the flames. Nothing happened although the cock was fully open. He stood for a moment at a loss, but a grunt from the fireman made him turn round. The extinguisher had disappeared in a mound of foam; it came to him that the rubber of the tube must be blocked, probably perished, he guessed, and that he was looking at leakage from loose fittings.

"Quick!" he yelled at the fireman. "Get me a spanner. Gotta get this bloody pipe off!"

The man disappeared hastily. Then David, acting on impulse, grabbed a small long handled scoop from a sandbox and began shovelling the wasted foam into the flaming area. This unorthodox method gradually began to pay dividends and he was thankful that leakage from the extinguisher was enough to satisfy his requirements. The rampant flames diminished somewhat as more foam was added, until eventually the burning fuel was smothered in its confined space. The fireman returned with a suitable implement but David knew the crisis was all but over. He checked that the foam had done its job, instructed the fireman to add more "just to be on the safe side!" then returned to the engineroom.

His eyes flicked across the various pressure gauges critically. He could see that the engine speed had been reduced to account for the reduced amount of steam available with the fuel shut off one boiler.

"Well done, Steve," he acknowledged to his assistant Steve Orme who had attended to the machinery in his absence.

Just then the telephone shrilled loudly. David wrenched it from its hook and barked into it: "Engineroom!"

"What the hell's going on? Why have we slowed down?" the Third Officer's normally calm voice was edged with a mixture of fear and anger.

David paused to clear his mind before answering, "No problem—we'll have her back to speed in a few minutes." It went against the grain to admit of crisis in the engineroom, if at all possible, as far he was concerned. He was about to hang up when a new voice came over the instrument. It was the Captain. "I want the engine back to full power immediately, do you hear me?"

The demand was delivered in tones that were not to be denied and David spluttered as he tried to explain himself. The other man was not in a mood to listen and repeated his order more forcibly. The phone went dead and David hung it up slowly with a feeling that he was in deep trouble.

"Oh well," he said resignedly to Orme, "let's get this lot sorted out. Himself seems a bit miffed."

CHAPTER 11

▼

Captain George Pilgrim cut a strange figure; he was extremely muscular but at the same time very short, giving him an almost square appearance. Somehow his height seemed scarcely more than the width of his shoulders. He had a broad head with straight brown hair swept back from the forehead. But it was his expression that most struck David Watson: it was not one of forgiveness. Indeed, he decided, the eyes staring unblinkingly at him were devoid of any feeling at all unless it was distaste.

It was early afternoon of the day following the fire in the boiler casing and David had been summoned to the bridge in company with the Chief Engineer. The cause of the conflagration had been established and with the flames extinguished the boiler had been returned to full operation. This had all happened before David's watch had been completed the previous evening and the actual loss of speed had not been great. Fortunately the convoy had not been at full speed so *Arthurian Castle* had soon regained her position. But George Pilgrim was not one to let the matter rest and hence David and Fraser McKay now stood ready to explain.

"So what the hell is going on down that engineroom of yours, Chief?"

McKay was not intimidated as he looked down at the shorter man. "We had a minor fire, sir. It was immediately and effectively dealt with by Mr. Watson. He is to be commended for his action in my view."

"I'll be the judge of who should be commended," growled Pilgrim. "Why was it necessary to slow down? Tell me that."

"David?" McKay nodded.

"Well, sir, I'm afraid the fireman fitted a clean burner without its pressure tip; instead of spraying fuel in a pressurised cloud it just splurged a lot of oil into the air supply trunking. Unfortunately this took fire and we couldn't put it out without shutting of the fuel supply to one boiler—hence the slight reduction of revs."

"Slight reduction of revs!" Pilgrim shouted the words with a rising inflexion. "We were losing the convoy hand over fist. Do you realise how dangerous it is to be without the protection of the warships? Eh? Boy!"

The Captain was working himself into a temper but David felt a need to explain himself further. Rather inadvisably he started to interrupt his superior.

"Sir, I was…"

Pilgrim exploded: "Don't speak while I'm speaking! In future you will not slow the main engine without the express permission of the bridge, is that clear?"

"Er, yes sir, but there was no time…"

"Is that clear, boy?" Pilgrim's lips were drawn in a thin line as he suppressed his anger.

"Yes, sir." David felt his own temper rising.

"Good, then leave my bridge and in future make sure your firemen know how to change burners correctly."

The interview was over and David turned to leave. Over his shoulder he could hear the Chief Engineer endeavouring to recover the situation, but to no avail. David felt unjustifiably slighted as clambered down the steel bridge ladders. In his heart he knew he was in the right but still the public dressing down in front of the lookout and helmsman, not to mention the Second Officer, had been like a blow to the body.

As his feet reached the boat deck he turned to the ship's rail, seeking a moment's solitude to gather his thoughts. He could see in the distance off the starboard quarter one of the aircraft carriers ploughing along at a somewhat greater speed than that of the convoy. His anger gradually subsided as he watched a flight of aircraft become airborne one after the other. They gathered into formation before turning over the stern of *Arthurian Castle*, heading eastward. David recognised the characteristic growl of Rolls Royce Merlin engines as the fighters, Sea Hurricanes, flew past. There had been rumours around the ship that German reconnaissance planes were already in contact with the convoy and he guessed the Sea Hurricanes would be on the lookout for any interlopers. He continued to watch the big carrier with her escorting cruiser for a few minutes before deciding to return to his cabin.

Suddenly there came a series of heavy dull thumps, four in all. David stood still, caught in indecision. The noises were unexplained yet reminded him frighteningly of the sounds he had heard aboard the U-boat when she had successfully fired torpedoes. The aircraft carrier, which he now recognised as *HMS Eagle*, seemed to be turning toward him but there was something odd about her. The turn was making the flight deck lean at an odd angle and she was also slowing down noticeably. The list increased until, to David's horror, he could see parked aircraft beginning to slide down the severe incline. As a Sea Hurricane fell into the sea with a huge splash he began to understand how serious the situation had become: *Eagle* had been torpedoed and was already in her death throes. There were tiny figures moving across the huge expanse of the flight deck that was now fully exposed as the great ship capsized. He could see men being flung or jumping into the water. He stood horrified, powerless to help as fellow seafarers perished before his eyes. With almost indecent haste the vessel subsided below the surface, taking many good men with her. It seemed almost as if he were the only witness as the convoy continued on its way leaving the disaster scene behind. David could hardly believe his eyes—did no one care? There were men swimming out there—was no one going to help them?

As if reading his thoughts he heard a soft voice at his side: "If we stop we'd be a sitting duck for the U-boat." Unnoticed, the Chief Engineer had joined him. "They'll send a couple of destroyers to investigate—try to find the sub. And also pick up survivors."

As if in response to the older man's words, a small warship travelling at high speed swept past them; another vessel could be seen on course to cross their stern. The two stood silently watching until *Arthurian Castle* had passed out of visual range. Eventually it was McKay who voiced the thought that was in both their minds.

"If they can so easily sink such a fine ship, what chance do we have?"

There was no answer that could be made and they separated without further discussion.

Down on the stern Fred Gates and his crew stood to at the 4-inch gun ready for any target that might offer itself. They would not be effective against high altitude bombers, but low flyers and submarines would be fair game. It was a long day and they knew there would be no rest before nightfall.

As it happened, the Italian Air Force decided to make its first attack on the convoy at dusk. A group comprising thirty Junkers Ju-88 bombers and six Heinkel 111 torpedo-bombers closed on the convoy from the port side. The escorting destroyers had deployed to a position further from the merchantmen as soon as the raiders had shown up on radar screens. It was intended that anti-aircraft fire should be directed at the Italians at the earliest opportunity in order to break up their formations. At the same time fighters could be seen lifting off the decks of the two remaining aircraft carriers, *HMS Indomitable* and *Victorious*.

Gates watched with professional interest as the attack developed. The sun was setting in a deep red glow as the guns commenced firing. Within seconds it seemed the sky was filled with thousands of tiny black puffy clouds as anti-aircraft shells exploded. Interspersing the black were the bright trails of tracer from the smaller calibre weapons zipping in all directions. As yet there was no sign of aircraft from Gates' vantage point at the stern of *Arthurian Castle*. The crash and crackle of gunfire was deafening and there could be little chance of hearing an aircraft engine at long range. The size of the convoy was such that there was a considerable distance between the point of attack at one side and Gates further back on the other.

He waited expectantly as the barrage continued unabated.

"Let's be ready now, you lot!" he yelled at his crew. "Like as not the buggers will come our way after they've dropped their loads!"

Suddenly he spotted the first marauder turning and climbing sharply over the line of merchantmen to port. He could see it was out of range and under fire from the closer ships. It disappeared from his line of sight. But soon more aircraft appeared; he recognised the twin radial engines of a Ju-88 flying toward them. It was flying low over the convoy either already damaged or trying to avoid gunfire. Fred gave orders and the 4-inch barked sharply but to no immediate effect. They fired again and then as they were reloading it disappeared into the gloom of advancing night.

There were more aircraft around them now, all fleeing the wrath of the anti-aircraft guns. There was a cheer from somewhere up amidships as a Ju-88 appeared, its wings on fire, plummeting vertically into the sea like some giant Catherine wheel. They got off a few more rounds without result but were heartened to see parachutes drifting toward the sea from another Junkers that had succumbed to the ferocious fleet barrage.

Then, as suddenly as it had begun, the battle was over. The guns fell silent. It was a relief to hear nothing more than the swish of the sea along the side and the rumble of the propeller beneath them.

"Well, lads, looks like we sent 'em 'ome wi' a flea in their ear!" averred Fred strongly.

The statement started off a bout of self-congratulation as the tension occasioned by the attack began to diminish. The jubilant gunners discussed the details of the shot down aeroplanes at length. Fred smiled at the chatter, aware that their input had been minimal, but enjoying the general euphoria nonetheless.

"Hey Fred, do you reckon they'll be back?" asked the baby-faced loader, Dick Stokes.

Gates laughed out loud at the ingenuous youngster. "I think we can bet on that. Mebbe not tonight but we've still a ways to go to get to Malta."

As it happened, the air raid would be regarded as no more than a probe; certainly the convoy emerged unscathed with some downed aircraft to their credit, but the wiser heads knew that much worse lay in the near future. They enjoyed an unmolested night and morale was high when the new day dawned. It was as well that the various crews had a restful night as their trials and tribulations started again just after breakfast when a group of nineteen Ju-88's attacked. Once again the anti-aircraft gunners were successful as six bombers were destroyed and the convoy steamed on undamaged.

They had something of a warning of the dangers that surrounded them during the morning when it was possible to see, albeit well astern, a long range Sunderland flying boat attacking a suspected submarine. They could not determine aboard *Arthurian Castle* whether the aeroplane had been triumphant, but Gates for one felt heartened by the event.

It was early afternoon when the next attack developed and this time it was a much more determined affair. The forces employed were still entirely those of the Italian Air Force; the first wave were Savoia Marchetti SM-84 bombers escorted by a squadron of obsolescent biplane fighters that were mainly shot down. A second wave of torpedo bombers and more SM-84's followed shortly afterward but the convoy defences proved more than adequate. The formations were split up by the English fighters and the merchantmen survived once more. But then the defenders' luck changed for the worse as the German Luftwaffe took a hand.

Flying from Sicily thirty-seven Junkers Ju-87 dive-bombers approached the mass of shipping. This was the aircraft that had cut swathes across Europe and Russia as the victorious German Army had advanced. Flown by an experienced crew, the Ju-87 Stuka was highly accurate in delivering its bomb load and had already demonstrated this effectiveness against the Royal Navy in the Mediterranean. Twelve aircraft that attacked the convoy's port wing penetrated the destroyer's screening barrage. The first Merchant Navy casualty resulted. Four bombs were aimed at the cargo ship *Deucalion*. There were three detonations very close alongside, but the final missile was a direct hit. It penetrated the deck, emerged through the ship's side above the water line and then exploded. *Deucalion* slowed dramatically and was quickly passed by succeeding ships. Despite grievous damage she was got under way again at reduced speed and continued on toward Malta in company with a destroyer. Unfortunately her heroic efforts were to come to nothing in the days ahead as she was attacked again and had to be abandoned.

As far as the gunners on the after deck of *Arthurian Castle* were concerned, the loss of one of their number came as a major disappointment after the earlier successes. Fred Gates shook his head in dismay as the damaged vessel disappeared from view astern.

"Come on lads, we'll just 'ave to shoot down more Jerries. Stop 'em coming back!"

There were a few smiles as the gun's crew settled into their routine once more, firing their gun at a retreating Junkers. The air raid was finally over. They were granted a brief respite. Fred surveyed the fleet through his binoculars carefully.

"Looks like the rest of us got away wi' it again. Take a breather, lads, it should be a while before they're back."

"How's it going, Fred?"

Gates swung around to find David Watson strolling toward him. "Wattie! We're fine, but you shouldn't be 'ere speshly wi'out a tin 'at."

"Thought I'd see how the other half lives. It's a bit eerie down the bottom of the engineroom. You can hear the guns of the fleet then every now and then this beauty shakes the place about as it fires." David slapped the breech of the 4-inch as he replied. "It seems like we're singled out for every attack and it's not so nice when a bomb explodes underwater. The ship's sides seem to magnify the noise."

"We've been lucky so far, it's mainly the port wing that's gettin' the pasting."

"Hang on, what's she up to?"

David pointed out across the stern at a destroyer steaming at full speed in the direction from which they had come. At length they heard a succession of dull explosions.

"Depth charges," commented Fred laconically.

There were more bangs before the Royal Naval vessel was lost to view.

"'Ope she got the bastard," came a voice from the gun's crew.

Later they were to see convincing evidence of the destroyer's success as she steamed past slowly, her bow heavily damaged after ramming and sinking an Italian submarine.

More air attacks were dealt with involving Italian dive-bombers and torpedo-carrying aircraft during the early evening. Then came the most significant attack of the whole day. Once again it was the German Stukas that were responsible. Twelve Ju-87's avoided the English fighters and braved the anti-aircraft barrage to concentrate on the modern aircraft carrier *HMS Indomitable*. Armed with 1000-pound bombs, they pressed home their attack resolutely. To the naked eye the mighty vessel vanished in a cloud of spray and smoke. For a while it seemed she must have been sunk, but then she reappeared, moving slowly and turning out of the convoy line. There had been two direct hits, one up forward near the lift and the other at the after lift. The flight deck was opened up over a huge area and internal damage, particularly on the hangar deck, was extensive as fires raged uncontrollably. A further three bombs narrowly missed the stricken vessel, causing more damage and some flooding. *Indomitable* was left circling painfully, many fine lives prematurely terminated. The ship was no longer a fighting force as far as the convoy was concerned and she was to have a difficult time withdrawing to the west and the safety of Gibraltar.

"What happens now?" asked David.

He and Fred Gates were sitting in the latter's cabin drinking a cup of cocoa; he had prepared the drinks in time to meet David as he came off watch and the two friends were quietly discussing the situation.

"Rumour has it the big stuff was always goin' to leave us about 'ere. Should be getting some air support from the Malta Spitfires soon so maybe she's done her job."

"I don't know about you but I feel a bit naked without those Hurricanes and the other fighters up there during the day!"

Fred sipped his cocoa reflectively. "Aye, yer right there, we'll miss 'em."

"I guess there will be a lot more damaged ships before this trip's over," concluded David. "Do you think there's any chance they'll abandon the voyage if we lose many more ships?"

"The way I hear it, Malta's close to starvation. Wi'out us they'll have to surrender. What do you think?"

"In that case I hope our luck holds out." David felt a coldness in his stomach as he considered their prospects. He shrugged and tried to push the feeling to one side.

CHAPTER 12

▼

Whatever else could she do? Megan let the facts of the situation rumble around in her mind. The route march from the beach had been mercifully short, given the physical frailty of the survivors. They had quickly arrived at a native village set back from the littoral along a well-trodden track. The reception had been cordial if complicated by lack of a common language and the group had slipped into village life happily. The problem was, as Megan saw it, that the acceptance of that life was too easy; and there were no meaningful discussions about moving on. It had been understandable in the first few weeks after their landing when they had needed to recover from the privations of the days in the lifeboat Those times had passed although Dick Rafferty was still suffering slightly from the effects of the blow to his head: the wound was taking longer to finally heal than she would have expected, although she was confident that provided she continued to change the dressing regularly there would be no major problems.

No, the need was to generate within her companions a wish to return to civilisation. She suspected that they viewed the village as a refuge from the dangers endemic in seafaring during a World War and that this was the major factor encouraging her companions to stay put. Rafferty remained the *de facto* leader of the group, now totalling just seven, and it was up to him to provide the impetus to leave the village. She resolved to have a serious talk with the young Third Officer when a suitable opportunity presented itself. Megan was determined to get home to Britain as soon as possible, but to do that she would need the whole-hearted support of her companions.

Her reverie was interrupted by one of the villagers. It was easy to consider the well-muscled six-foot native as the leader of the tiny community. The man's presence was tangible, like some transparent cloak and he always became involved in any discussions with the Europeans. Through his orders they had been given an old house in which to live. Built of rough chopped wood and roofed with a thatch of rotten foliage from the surrounding jungle, the building was flattered by being termed a house: it did represent, however, a dry, if rank smelling, haven of sufficient size to accommodate all the survivors. In short, in a strange land, it represented home.

Megan smiled at the native whose black face split toothily in a reciprocal gesture. There followed a difficult dialogue mainly consisting of hand signals and drawings in the dust at their feet, punctuated by words in a language she did not understand. Her role as spokesperson had been established at an early stage and it was now quite natural for her to be approached.

She sensed the present interchange had a particular importance and concentrated the harder as a result. Yet the significance evaded her for some minutes. There was a clear reference to food, a not difficult concept to get across, and then something more general. There was the dim stirring of comprehension when she was startled by a word she recognised as the man gabbled in frustration. Staring hard at the man she repeated it back to him, "Allez?"

Another broad grin appeared on the dark features, "Oui, Allez."

Megan was momentarily tongue tied as she digested the fact that the man knew French. Her own knowledge of that language was not extensive but she plied him with a few phrases nonetheless. The results were far from spectacular but at least it became possible for her to confirm the message the villager wanted to impart.

It was simple, really, and rather obvious with hindsight: there was a limit to the amount of food available to the community and the villagers simply could not continue to feed their visitors. In a way Megan was pleased; here was reason to move, the lever, the motivation she had been seeking. She thanked the man for his message, trying to reassure him at the same time that his request would be met. He nodded and left.

As she watched his departing back, Megan had a fleeting moment of unexplained concern occasioned by the man's smattering of French. She put it to one side, bent on searching out the various survivors in order to explain the new situation.

"So let's get this straight," said John Davies some time later, his soft Welsh lilt hardened in anger. "His Nibs wants us out?"

"I'm afraid he does. I don't believe its personal but there will be a shortage of food for the village if we stay longer. There's probably a limit to how much they can grow, particularly in the coming winter…" Megan let the words hang in the air, almost daring the Third Engineer to argue.

It was one of the other engineers who broke the ensuing silence. "But where will we go?"

Megan felt herself relax slightly, realising that at least one of the group had unconsciously accepted the need to leave. When she had gathered the men together she had known it would be difficult to get them to make the decision to quit the village and tailored her explanation accordingly. She had been careful to maintain her role as spokesperson rather than appear to be leading them but had phrased her elucidation in such a way that there was only one logical conclusion that could be drawn.

Dick Rafferty, silent to this point, judged the moment for his intervention to perfection. "There must be a town, at least, maybe even a proper port, somewhere along the coast."

There was a murmur of begrudging agreement.

"I think we should send out a scouting party with rations for say a week. They could follow the coast and return. If nothing is found travelling south we could repeat the exercise with another lot going north. What do you think?"

Accepting the inevitable Davies spoke for all as he asked, "Who were you thinking of sending?"

"I thought you and three others, your choice as to whom," replied Rafferty gratefully seizing the initiative.

The next day the four-strong party left with the good wishes of Megan, Rafferty and the greaser Tom Edwards. There was an element of sadness as the survivors were further split but Davies, now committed to the success of his mission, confidently predicted that he would be back within the week. As the quartet disappeared along a coastal path Megan hoped the confidence was not misplaced.

Her concern was well directed. Davies and his cohorts never returned. Life in the village continued more or less unchanged for a week, then she found herself spending more and more time in the vicinity of the seashore looking in vain for the foragers. After ten days she began to accept privately that they were not coming back. At the end of a fortnight she and the two men agreed that an alternative plan would have to be implemented.

"I guess we've got no option but to try the opposite route, go north," stated Edwards.

"You're probably right," agreed Rafferty. "I can't think that Davies would have just abandoned us if he had found civilisation."

"Mayhap he found some locals who weren't as friendly as our lot."

There really was not a lot more to be said on the subject and they agreed to gather together as much food as was practicable and strike off to the north early the next morning.

The village headman helped by providing coarse loose-weave sacks into which were stored yams and a variety of fresh fruit together with a small quantity of cooked rice. There were also a couple of hollow gourds containing fresh water that Edwards offered to carry. By the time they were ready to leave it was well past midday, Rafferty's hoped for early start somehow not having been achieved. They were taking their leave of the villagers when a faint rumble of noise was borne into them on a slight breeze.

"Did you hear that?" asked Rafferty anxiously.

"Aye, that's a diesel engine," replied Edwards.

"Saved by the bell, eh?" Dick was all smiles.

Megan said nothing. Somehow the sound, clearly distinguishable now from the ceaseless chatter of the surrounding jungle, held an element of menace for her. They sat waiting expectantly. Eventually a small truck edged its way into the centre of the village, its cab bestrewn with bits of vegetation in mute testimony to the narrowness of the trail it had followed. She looked doubtfully at the Renault badge on the vehicle's blunt radiator. It stopped and a figure stepped down on the passenger's side. It was not possible to see the driver against the sun's glare on the windscreen but he remained seated.

Megan concentrated on the newcomer. He was middle aged, seemingly tending to fat and dressed in a crumpled white suit. He approached, lifted a broad brimmed white hat in salutation, then stopped to examine them.

"Are we glad to see you," said Rafferty effusively.

The man stared, a bead of sweat rolling down his face.

"We were just about to hike up north looking for civilisation."

There was still no comment from the visitor.

Rafferty burbled on, giving a potted history of the loss of *Petrain Castle* and the voyage of the lifeboat. Finally his diatribe was interrupted as the stranger raised his palm imperiously.

"Welcome to the Ivory Coast," the voice was high pitched and the English heavily accented. "My name is LeBrun. I represent the Vichy French government of this territory. You will consider yourself internees for the remainder of the war." As he spoke he gestured to the lorry and was soon joined by a party of armed coloured soldiers who surrounded the three survivors.

Megan felt a sudden sadness suffuse her consciousness as she realised that any hopes of seeing England again in the short term had just been cruelly dashed.

CHAPTER 13

▼

The day started to go sour as it approached its conclusion, both for the convoy and *Arthurian Castle*. As David was doing his machinery inspection prior to taking over the watch from the Second Engineer, he noticed drips of water coming from the insulation lagging around one of the main steam pipes. It was the supply for the main engine and the extent of the problem was obscured by the lagging.

He mentioned the matter to his predecessor at the handover of the watch and was told to keep an eye on it. They both knew that there was not a lot that could be done whilst the ship was at full speed. "Keeping an eye on it" was really a shorthand means of saying "Let's hope it doesn't get any worse before we get into port."

Almost before the Second Engineer had left the engineroom there came a series of severe percussions punching heavy vibrations through the steel plates of the hull. David jumped visibly at the harsh shocks, instantly aware that he was yet again hearing torpedoes finding targets close by. It would be some time before he learned that in those four impacts a couple of cruisers and the all-important tanker, *Ohio*, had been heavily damaged. Standing on the platform adjacent to the engine controls well below the waterline was suddenly the last place in the world he wanted to be; David found himself gripping the main steam valve handwheel, his knuckles white. Across the engineroom he caught the eye of his assistant. Steve Orme looked petrified. The stare was rudely interrupted as the telegraph clanged insistently. Automatically David swung the big handwheel watching the revolutions decline as he reduced the steam to the engine. The action helped him get a grip on his fear and he smiled at Orme.

"They must be getting excited up on the bridge!" he shouted.

The telegraph rang a second time. He closed the valve and watched the heavy engine connecting rods cycle to a stop.

"Check the boiler water levels, Steve," he called, anxious to divert the lad's imagination away from the torpedo strikes.

There were more telegraph orders that he complied with efficiently, wondering what was causing the flurry of activity. Normal convoy station keeping required just small speed changes and it was very unusual for the bridge to signal a complete stop even for a short time. Being unable to see what was going on on the surface of the sea, the role of the engineer was necessarily one of blind obedience. The problem was that men tended to imagine all sorts of things born of external sounds and bridge orders. Perhaps a torpedo had been aimed at *Arthurian Castle* and the slow down had been necessary to avoid it: perhaps the next one might not be seen in time to take avoiding action…

Above the thrashing thunder of the engine now back to full speed, David caught the sound of the ship's whistle screeching. The revolutions fell slightly before recovering and he guessed this was a reaction to an extreme helm movement. There was a slight canting of the plates under his feet, then they were level again.

Orme appeared at his elbow. "Must be trying to avoid bumping into something!"

David stared at him sombrely. "Could be."

Orme suddenly looked sick as it dawned on him what he had said.

"How's that boiler water, Steve?"

"Oh, er, fine. I think I'll just check the propeller shaft bearings, okay?"

"Yeah, do that—and whilst you're on your rounds, have a look at the main steam pipe leakage. All these speed changes won't be doing it much good."

"Right, I'm on my way," responded Orme. "Hell, I wish we knew what was going on up top."

As it happened he was not alone in that thought, yet Fred Gates was on deck and able to scan the surrounding sea. The problem was that, in the twilight as the sun dipped below the horizon, it was extremely difficult to decide exactly what was going on. Ships had been torpedoed and had slowed, falling out of line as they did so; succeeding vessels had had to take avoiding action. The convoy being ordered to make an emergency change of course compounded the result. The cohesion of the group of ships was broken; the beginnings of confusion began to set in as individual masters conned their commands as best they could in the circumstances but without much concern for their correct position in the convoy.

The enemy seized this moment to mount another air raid. The escorts' anti-aircraft barrage erupted once more with a mind numbing blast of sound. The rattle of short-range weaponry counter pointed by the regular thump of the multiple pom-poms; the whole underwritten by the deeper more measured thunder of the heavier secondary armament of the capital ships. Gates caught a glimpse of a Stuka falling almost vertically toward a ship ahead, its Jumo engine howling as it accelerated. The aircraft began to pull out of its dive just as a bomb peeled away from its underside. It recovered to level flight close to *Arthurian Castle* and was immediately engaged by the quick firing guns deployed close to the bridge. There was no discernible effect as the pilot turned away to safety.

Fred nodded across to his loader. "Stay awake, there'll be some low level stuff as well after these Stukas." There was a tacit understanding that they could not engage the dive-bombers with the elevation limitations of the big 4-inch gun. They knew it was fitted mainly to attack surfaced U-boats but they were not going to miss any opportunity to defend the ship in an air raid.

There was a huge explosion from up ahead and it was possible to see a merchant ship plainly silhouetted in the flames that were beginning to engulf it. Over the next few minutes there were other apparent successes for the bombers although it was not possible to see which vessels had been hit. It was a grim night for the convoy by now entering the most difficult phase of its journey to Malta. Fred's predictions were soon borne out as more aircraft were sighted on the port beam flying close to the water. They were Heinkel 111 torpedo bombers. As he watched lines of tracer converged on the attackers looking like streams of fireflies as they criss-crossed the darkening sky. The effectiveness or otherwise of their attack was lost to Fred, however, as a gaggle of Junkers 88's swept in and offered a viable target for the 4-inch crew. They fired regularly as long as their gun could be made to bear; unfortunately there were restrictions in training forward a gun mounted aft on a ship at the tail of the convoy.

The battle had now begun to involve *Arthurian Castle* much more; her armament, minimal though it was, was in almost continuous action as aircraft roared past. There were ships all around fighting for their lives and the careful formation of the convoy was a thing of the past. No longer were the Navy able to stop the raids reaching the vulnerable merchantmen. Warships and freighters were hit indiscriminately; some lay stopped and dying whilst others struggled on gallantly heavily damaged and at reduced speeds.

Out of the gloom flashed a Junkers 88 headed directly for them with its bomb doors open. Gates felt the deck cant as the ship turned to throw off the bomb aimer's calculations. The marauder jinked across the sky as the pilot lined up his machine again. The air around it was live with tracer fire but yet it bore in on the ship. There was a brief sparkle across the starboard engine cowling as some of the anti-aircraft fire took effect but the Junkers maintained its course. Fred, looking forward through binoculars, held his breath as he saw two bombs leave the plane headed, it seemed, directly for the bridge. The ship was still turning and for an instant Fred hoped that luck was going to be on their side. But the aircraft was too low and too close to its victim to miss. The first bomb ploughed into the hatchcoaming around No.2 hold exploding with a huge flash of flame. The blast largely dissipated itself across the deck, with jagged fragments of metal crashing into winches, derricks and the forward deckhouse. The main superstructure under the bridge was penetrated in a dozen places and three crew cabins were wrecked. A measure of good fortune still clung to the ship, as the spaces were unoccupied at the moment of impact. Much more serious though was the hole ripped in the deck by the explosion: it exposed the cargo and at the same time white-hot shards of steel became buried in the packaging of the freight.

The second bomb slammed directly into the bridge housing, burst through the thin plating and came to rest in the officers' dining saloon. By some fluke it did not explode but lay there rocking slightly to the movement of the merchant-man, its crumpled fins entangled in the wreckage of a heavy wooden table. The room was empty and surprisingly it would be some time before the bomb was discovered. The lack of a detonation had led to an assumption on the bridge that it had bounced over the side. The ship was still under attack, fighting for its life and there was simply no time available to check the second missile.

The first successful attack on *Arthurian Castle* seemed to attract further bombers as if they scented her incipient weakness. A twin-engined Junkers flashed by, its bombs exploding in the water close alongside the still turning ship. Gates heard the clang of metal on metal as splinters cracked the side. There would be holes and leakage thereabouts and he could only hope that major structural damage would be avoided. A third aircraft was above them shearing away without dropping its bomb load as a lucky Oerlikon burst from amidships chewed through its port aileron.

"Look out, Fred," shouted the loader as another aeroplane attacked, this time from astern.

The gun barked sharply as they managed to get a round away. The aiming was hurried and their shell missed; but the Junkers' pilot, alarmed by the flame of the gun's firing, thumbed the button on his control column. A line of bright tracer reached out for the stern of *Arthurian Castle*. It seemed to move slowly at first, then accelerated rapidly, drawn inexorably to the 4-inch. Fred ducked behind the breech but the bullets flicked away over his head without finding any targets. He breathed a sigh of relief as a thundering dark shape screamed over his head. He could see the blackness between open bomb bay doors but no missiles were released.

"Look out, 'e'll turn for another go!" he yelled at his crew.

They hastily trained around trying to track the German but it vanished into the gloom without returning.

A final bomber attacked from ahead but it was already on fire in the port engine, having been hit by one of the escorts. The quick firing guns engaged it. Their efforts were immediately successful as hits were seen along the fuselage. Fred found himself cheering as the mortally wounded aircraft turned away even before it reached a position from which to release its bombs. It was hit again but despite rough sounding engines it continued to fly until it was out of range.

"'E'll not make it back to Sicily." He pronounced judgement with great satisfaction before turning around in puzzlement. It took several seconds to register what was wrong: there was a developing quietness as the guns gradually fell silent. Not just aboard *Arthurian Castle* but also around the convoy. The raid was over.

The 4-inch's crew were spread around their charge sometime after midnight drinking cups of cocoa when Gates heard a familiar voice.

"How's it going, Fred?"

"Wot you doin' 'ere, Wattie?"

"Come to see how the other half lives. Mind you, I wouldn't mind knowing what's been going on the last few hours. All we hear in the engineroom is the bumps and bangs!" David lowered himself onto the deck to sit alongside Gates.

Fred proceeded to give David a rather lurid account of the air raid ably assisted by comments from his crew. He managed to make the explosion of the bomb appear as just another minor event. It was suggested with tongue firmly in cheek that the might of the Luftwaffe had descended on *Arthurian Castle* only to be firmly rebuffed by her gunners, principally those gathered around the 4-inch. David laughed at the descriptions and not in the least misled by the claims of success.

Eventually Gates ran out of words.

"So, just how many planes did you actually shoot down?" asked David innocently.

There was a brief pause; then Fred chuckled, "We sure as 'ell frightened a couple!"

David couldn't help smiling at the Cockney's comment and soon the four gunners joined him in a tension-relieving gust of laughter. The stress of the brief action had left each man thankful to have survived but fearing the return of the attackers.

"I suppose you'll be standing down now the bombers have gone? Getting your head down in your hammocks?"

"That's what we thought, an' all," replied Fred grumpily' "Unfortunately the bridge think otherwise. Seems there may be enemy ships around. No, we'll be sleepin' 'ere for the foreseeable, I reckon. Anyway, what you doin' still in yer boiler suit? No shower and beddy-byes?"

"'Fraid not, we've got a wee steam leak in the engineroom and Chiefie wants to have a go at stopping it when we have a quiet spell. In fact I'd best be off now before you start ambushing the whole Italian Navy with that pea shooter of yours." David stood up wearily.

"We ain't gonna stop are we?" the loader Hempel was shocked at the thought.

"No, don't worry. We could be scalding in steam down there and the Captain would still expect us to keep the engine up to power." David strolled off toward the central accommodation area and the engineroom access watertight door. He had deliberately understated the extent of the leak. The truth of the matter was that the violent speed changes required by the bridge as they sought to manoeuvre the ship away from danger had tended to exacerbate the problem. The damaged joint was prone to expansion and contraction as steam flowed at different rates to the main engine. To make matters worse the shock of bombs exploding on board and alongside had shaken the structure stressing the pipe still further. The drips of water had now become a steady hiss of escaping steam.

David could see two boiler-suited engineers bending over the steam line as he stepped back into the machinery space. They were outlined by a cloud of vapour.

"Ah, David, thanks for coming back down," Chief Engineer McKay nodded amiably. "I'm going to try to wedge between the flanges: at least it will reduce the leakage rate."

With the insulation removed two steel pipes were exposed. They were covered in a light scale of rust and joined by individual flanges bolted solidly together. In normal operation the asbestos fibre joint between the flanges would have ensured steam tightness. But these were far from normal times and *Arthurian Castle* was overdue for repairs. The joint had failed in one tiny area, allowing steam to blow past. This initial area was growing rapidly as more fibre was eroded. In a matter of hours it would fail completely; whatever Captain Pilgrim might say there would be no alternative in that event other than to stop to make a full repair.

McKay donned a pair of thick asbestos gloves. The other engineer, Steve Orme, handed him a hammer and a small 'V'-shaped strip of copper ground with a taper at its tip. The sliver of metal was inserted at the leakage point and with a clean blow of the hammer driven hard between the flanges. McKay delivered further blows as the steam was deflected but not diminished by the thin copper.

"Right, give me another one," he gestured at Orme.

The heat rising from the pipes was intense and all three men were sweating profusely. Orme handed the second wedge over but this time McKay failed to place it accurately due to the leakage cloud. As he struck with the hammer the copper jammed against the rim of the flange and buckled uselessly.

"Damn," snarled McKay in frustration.

The three men struggled for another half-hour taking it in turns to work with the hammer in close proximity to the steam jet. Eventually the leakage was reduced to a gentle whiffle. There was now little more that could be done except hope that the temporary expedient would last until they reached Malta.

"Well done, lads," said McKay as they secured the insulation back into place around the repair.

David and Orme climbed slowly up the steel ladders on the way out of the engineroom.

"Think it will last?" Orme's face was bright pink, his boiler suit dark with its saturation of sweat.

"God knows! Just pray that it does…I don't fancy stopping around here for a major repair." David tried to sound confident but without too much success. Orme peered at him worriedly yet offered no comment.

They emerged into a small alleyway running forward past the engineer's cabins and were immediately pushed aside by a group of men carrying a huge roll of tarpaulin.

"Gangway, gangway!" yelled the leader, a heavyset individual; Connell was ship's bosun and a very competent seaman.

"What's up, Bose?" queried Orme.

"Bomb damage up forward," came the reply shouted over a departing shoulder.

The bosun hurried his party onto the forward deck, cursing the unwieldy bulk of the canvas. He shouted orders and the roll was hurriedly spread across the deck and gradually manhandled into place across the gaping hole. The sailors were just finishing lashing the cover in place and might have noticed a tiny tendril of smoke curling up from the cargo hold but abruptly an enormous thunderclap reverberated back from the bow. The whole ship shook violently, her stern rearing out of the sea under the force of the explosive percussion. A towering wall of water reared over the foc's'le crashing down angrily and washing three flailing sailors across the deck. There was a cry of anguish as a seaman reached out despairingly for support, missed a stanchion, then slid quickly through the shipside rails and vanished in the blackness.

Arthurian Castle slowed to a stop. Suddenly out of the night came the first glimpse of their attacker; an Italian motor torpedo boat, having been successful with its torpedo launch, rushed in toward the ship's side, turning as it came. From its stern vivid tracer split the darkness. The aim was good and sailors staggering to their feet after the impact of the torpedo were mown down in a vicious hail of bullets. Connell threw himself behind the covering bulk of a cargo winch but the E-boat was past. The gunner had shifted his aim and was now raking the bridge with a withering fire. The racket of exploding shells filled the air. Then, as quickly as it came, the aggressor vanished into the night but Connell could still hear its engine and knew it would return. His memory retained a fleeting picture of the boat and he realised that its torpedo racks were empty. He was distracted by a moan from his right. He turned to see a bloody hand curl around a cast iron cleat and tense. A wiry body dragged itself into view. A head appeared briefly, then the figure rolled into the space alongside Connell.

He regarded a dirty blood streaked face, finally recognising John Oakes from his tarpaulin-rigging team.

"Keep your head down, the bastard'll be back!"

He'd no sooner spoken than they heard the strident rattle of gunfire once more. This time the tearing cloth sound of a machine gun was augmented by the slower *thump thump* of a larger calibre weapon. But the E-boat had lost the element of surprise and a Hotchkiss opened up immediately from the bridge wing in reply. The other weapons quickly followed suit. It was a furious if poorly directed response yet it served to upset the aim of the Italian gunners. The attacker slewed away after suffering slight damage to her tiny bridge structure. This time it continued on a reciprocal course to *Arthurian Castle* passing close to the stern where Fred Gates and his team were waiting.

The 4-inch cracked and a shell hit the torpedo boat at almost point blank range just forward of the stern. For an instant nothing happened; then a tongue of flame appeared at the point of impact. The boat slowed noticeably but still held steerageway as it disappeared once again into the night. Fred gazed out at the orange glow that bespoke their success as it gradually dwindled. Suddenly it flared brightly and the dull crump of an explosion rolled across the water. The flame died.

"Think we can claim that'un, lads?" he said with satisfaction.

Up on the foredeck Bosun Connell warily stood up, looked around, then heaved Oakes to his feet. They were the only survivors of the group that had been there when the attack developed.

"Let's have a look at that arm of yours," he spoke quietly, still coming to terms with the suddenness and ferocity of the attack.

CHAPTER 14

▼

Arthurian Castle got under way again shortly after dawn. She moved ponderously through the water, deliberately kept to a slow pace by a concern for the weakness of the bow. Although the torpedo had severely damaged the forefoot, the collision bulkhead, the heavy gauge steel wall that ran across the ship isolating the cargo spaces, remained intact. There was no leakage into the hold areas and it was hoped that once the bulkhead had been shored up internally they would be able to resume something approaching full speed. The Chief Officer, Brian Crawshaw, had been lowered on a rope from the fo'c'sle head to assess the damage externally. It appeared as though the Italian torpedo had had an incorrect depth setting. The plating was ripped away for twelve feet along the starboard side and slightly less on the other. Surprisingly most of the destruction was at or above the water line. It was alarming to gaze from one side of the ship to the other through the steel structure but in fine weather at least, they would be safe to continue onwards.

This was the message he had given to Captain Pilgrim after his overside foray. The Captain had been doubtful, suggesting that it might be better to turn round and head back to Gibraltar. Crawshaw had been totally dismissive of such a decision. Seeing that Pilgrim was shaken by the events of the night, the Mate had adopted a confident stance maintaining that from a seamanship point of view they were fit to continue. Eventually Pilgrim had agreed to continue. Crawshaw had been mildly surprised by the man's diffidence but had put it down to the aftermath of the E-boat attack.

Now that they were steaming again Crawshaw left the foredeck and returned to the bridge. He stared at the devastation of the once neat well-ordered space. In many respects the attack had been more successful here than at the bow. A hail of bullets had laid waste to the space. The windows had been blasted into myriad shards of flying glass that had raked the area. The Second Officer had absorbed a mass of splinters and died instantly. His sorely disfigured body lay in a pool of congealed blood at the front of the bridge. A further lifeless torso lay slumped to one side of the steering wheel. The helmsman had been unlucky to receive a machine-gun bullet through the temple as he stood at his post. Crawshaw swallowed quickly, feeling revolted by the carnage and made his way across the wooden floor.

"How are you feeling, Three-Oh?" he addressed the hunched figure of Colin Beck leaning heavily on the remains of a window frame.

"I'll get by," said Beck, grimacing slightly as he shifted his right arm painfully in a voluminous linen sling. A flesh wound from a sliver of glass had bled profusely before it could be attended to and he was feeling weak as a result. Beck knew, however, how lucky he had been to be standing behind the Second Mate at the change of the night watch. Another foot to one side and he would also be a bloody remnant on the floor.

"I'll relieve you once we know how much other hull damage exists."

"Fine, it's not exactly busy around here." Beck gestured toward the empty horizon, the convoy long departed.

"By the way, the steering telemotor's developed a leak. Can you warn Mr. McKay we'll need an engineer up here sometime during the day?"

"Sure," replied Crawshaw. "I'll let him know on my way down aft."

Gradually life aboard *Arthurian Castle* returned to something near normal on that bright August morning. Then the bomb was found. It should of course have been discovered much sooner but with so much damage to be dealt with elsewhere in the ship the dining room had been temporarily overlooked. It was not a particularly large device and its entry hole had initially been attributed to debris from the explosion of the first missile on the foredeck. Meals were being taken informally as repair and clean up work allowed. Eventually a steward was detailed to tidy the officer's dining saloon. He pulled upended chairs to one side to reach the broken table lying drunkenly against a bulkhead. It was jammed, refusing to move despite his vigorous efforts. He called for assistance and with three pairs of hands dragging at one end, the recalcitrant piece of furniture suddenly shifted. After the initial resistance was overcome it scraped across the floor easily.

The bomb was black and sinister looking as it moved slightly to the ship's motion, constrained only by its crushed guidance fins. There was no mistaking what it was and the room emptied rapidly. Over the next half-hour a procession of people, including the various department heads, paused at the saloon door. Nobody, whether drawn by curiosity or duty, stayed for long. It was impossible to know whether the thing was a dud or perhaps time delayed. Most people believed that it just required to be jarred sufficiently to release the erstwhile ineffective impact fuse. But the biggest problem was the lack of knowledge; even the naval gunners had no expertise that could be tapped. Was the bomb likely to explode or not? A shiver of fear ran through the men of Arthurian Castle. It was more than the worry of an explosion; it was the fear of the unknown.

On the bridge wing a small group discussed the matter.

"The question is, will it explode and, if so, when?" George Pilgrim was sweating profusely, yet his face looked unnaturally pale.

Fraser McKay shrugged dismissively. "There's no way of knowing. I reckon we just take it with us!"

"Don't be stupid, man," expostulated Pilgrim. "It could kill us all. We must turn back...find a Navy ship...they'll know what to do."

McKay frowned. "I don't think..."

"Judging by the damage caused by the first bomb, if it did go off it shouldn't be fatal as far as the ship's concerned," Crawshaw interrupted smoothly and authoritatively, his hand lightly placed on McKay' shoulder.

"That's as maybe, but I've got men's lives to think about. It's far too dangerous to continue," Pilgrim spoke loudly but somehow seemed to be looking for agreement from the other two.

"I was thinking of the lives on Malta and how many will be lost without food," replied the Mate. There was a murmur of support from McKay.

Pilgrim started to bluster but Crawshaw interrupted once more. "I think we can do something to reduce the risk to the crew."

"Oh, aye? And what might that be, I ask?"

Crawshaw outlined his plan to enthusiastic support from the Chief Engineer.

Captain Pilgrim remained doubtful but in the face of the confidence of his senior officers was forced to concede. He nodded briefly. "If anything changes I want to know immediately. If that thing starts ticking..." The sentence was left unfinished as he strode off to stand at the limit of the bridge wing near the ship's side.

"I'll get the Bosun started straight away, Chiefie," said Crawshaw.

"Aye, fine. I'll see if we can spare a couple of hands from the engineroom. Might speed things up a bit!"

David Watson was wakened unwillingly from a deep sleep by a wheezing rumble of machinery. He crawled from his bunk, scratching his head, irritably wondering why, in the middle of a voyage, a deck winch was being operated. Having slipped into some clothes, he wandered out on deck. The hatch covers had been removed from No.4 cargo hold and a bundle of sacks of flour supported in a wide mesh rope net were in the process of being lifted. The winch rattled importantly gushing steam from a leaky gland. There were shouts of guidance; then flour was gently lowered onto the deck alongside the hold. A party of sailors quickly removed the sacks and then disappeared into the accommodation area with their loads. Intrigued, David tagged along behind the last man. He was surprised to find the flour being passed into the dining saloon. There was already a substantial pile of sacks dominating the room, clearly placed for a particular purpose although it was not immediately obvious to him what that might be.

"Come to give us a hand?" It was the Mate, Crawshaw, standing at his elbow.

"Uh, no, er, I mean, what's going on?"

Crawshaw smiled humourlessly. "No one mentioned our super-cargo?"

David was nudged toward the opposite side of the flour bag wall. He stared at the black bomb casing in gradually dawning understanding. The missile was almost entirely surrounded by a three-foot thick cocoon that limited its movement and shielded the space from any explosive effect.

He turned away thinking about the practicalities of the protective screen, too involved to be frightened.

"That's okay for in here and above, but what about underneath? If that thing goes off it'll blast the deck apart."

Crawshaw nodded. "We checked the plans. We think its above No2 hold, which extends below us as far as the boiler-room bulkhead. Any detonation should be absorbed in the cargo."

"Should be," repeated David.

The Mate shrugged. "Nothing is ever perfect."

David drifted off seeking some breakfast before going on watch. His mind remained focused on the explosive device, trying to imagine the effect of the fuse suddenly activating. He considered various possibilities. The heart could be blown out of the ship if the bomb was powerful enough, but with no way of gauging that power he settled for something which made him feel fairly comfortable. He conjured up a vision of the flour absorbing the blast, of sacks blown apart, of flour dust billowing around the accommodation. He smiled to himself as he completed the fantasy with a thought of Captain Pilgrim emerging from the cloud indignantly thrashing at his normally impeccable uniform in a vain attempt to dislodge the fine powder.

The morning went well for *Arthurian Castle* as the effects of the night action were gradually dealt with. Speed was increased to eight knots and the Mate declared himself satisfied with the collision bulkhead after it had been strengthened with wooden shores. There was no sign of the convoy ahead, of course, due to its much greater speed. Oddly, although the fact was missed by everyone, there was no sign of any other damaged shipping despite the explosions that had illuminated the previous night.

Sottotenente di Vascello Aldo Fulgoni was angry. The damage to his precious command, Mas. 761 caused by a single British shell was enough justification of itself for his fury, yet in his heart he knew most of his anger was directed at himself. The momentary stupidity that had led to him taking the torpedo boat within the arc of fire of the merchantman's gun still troubled him deeply. He had been so intent in attacking the ship's bridge in a high-speed approach that he had omitted to order a change of course in time. Fulgoni stared bleakly at the charred timbers of the after deck of Mas.761. The shell had exploded in contact with a steel fitting just aft of the base of the quick-firer on the afterdeck. The gun was still operable although its original crew had been cut to pieces by splinters. Unfortunately spare, partially filled, fuel drums had been punctured by shrapnel. The gushing fluid had ignited and scoured the area with a sheet of flame. Only immediate action had avoided a complete disaster. Fulgoni had ordered a water spray to be applied to the fire. Normally water applied to an oil fire would simply have spread the problem, but his luck had been in as the source of the fire, the fuel, had been washed over the side. The resulting damage was largely cosmetic but looked far worse. Nonetheless he did not look forward to explaining to his Flotilla Commander why he had gone into action without emptying the drums into his below deck tanks and then jettisoning them. He was well aware that he and his crew had been extremely fortunate: the single round from the Britisher could well have caused the end of his command.

It had taken some hours to make his command seaworthy again after the fire, but they were now under way again toward their Sicilian base for repairs. Progress was deliberately slow as the E-boat was now short of fuel. Fulgoni sighed as he swept the horizon with his binoculars, remembering the unfortunate events of the night before. At least he would be able to report that one of his torpedoes had found a target. It remained a mystery as to why the second projectile that he had fired had missed, although he had a suspicion that it might have failed to keep to its pre-set depth. After consulting his chart, he ordered a course change and set-tled down to studying the surrounding sea once more. It was early afternoon when he again sighted *Arthurian Castle*. Surprised to find an unescorted cargo ship so far from the convoy, he didn't immediately recognise his earlier prey. The vessel seemed to be following a course that would lead her somewhat to the north of the bulk of her compatriots. This puzzled Fulgoni but he ignored the thought as he pressed the alarm button to alert his ship's company.

The gun crews closed up at their weapons as the E-boat came up to full power and swept into the attack. Without torpedoes, Fulgoni knew that he would have to use the quick-firer to punch holes in the freighter's side if he were going to sink her. Mas.761 accelerated to over thirty knots rapidly overtaking her quarry in order to be able to make an attack from ahead.

The insistent ringing of alarm bells reverberated through the accommodation as David Watson and Steve Orme made their way up the stairway leading to the bridge. Between them they carried a bag of tools and a can of hydraulic fluid.

"What now?" asked Watson without pausing in his climb.

They had been detailed to deal with a leak on the bridge steering mechanism at the completion of their morning watch. Stepping onto the bridge, it was possi-ble to see the Captain and Third Officer standing on the wing looking out over the port side. There was a shouted order and the helmsman spun his wheel hard. *Arthurian Castle* lurched into a turn to port. Another order, another wheel move-ment and the turn was completed. Suddenly the two officers threw themselves to the deck planking as the side rail disappeared in a cloud of wooden splinters. From a distance there came the rippling sound of rapid gunfire. The bridge area was filled with the sound of angry buzzing hornets, a sound that baffled David until he heard the impact of machine gun bullets on the steel structure. He pulled Orme to the relative shelter of the chart space at the rear of the bridge. They hud-dled together on the wooden deck.

"Do you think we picked a bad time to come up here?" He looked at Orme wryly.

"Maybe its not so bad in the engineroom after all," came the slightly shaky reply.

There was a shouted order and the ship heeled to another course change. They could hear the ship's own armament firing from the pits built around the bridge. There were dull thumping sounds resounding through the hull as the torpedo boat sprayed 40-mm canon shells along with the machine gun rounds. The gun-fire ceased abruptly as the attacker sheared off. Sensing that the danger was temporarily past, David stood up and glanced out at the sea. It was apparent to him that Captain Pilgrim was swinging his command to bring it stern on to the E-boat so that the 4-inch could be brought to bear. *Arthurian Castle* continued to swing through a broad arc but the vastly greater speed and agility of the motor-boat negated the ploy. The fast moving craft bore in again from dead ahead as her prey committed to her turn presented the broad extent of her side. Mas.761, her pennant numbers now clearly readable at her bow, twitched slightly to port and recommenced firing.

The return fire was accurate and effective. David watched as Oerlikon shells exploded along the upper works of the other craft. An Italian sailor was flung to the deck, an uncontrolled flapping of already lifeless limbs. The motorboat slowed suddenly as the body crashed into the engine controls shifting the lever for the port engine. But it was only a momentary lapse; the corpse was levered out of the way and speed restored. Yet this problem coupled with the continuing turn of the merchant ship enabled Fred Gates and his men to begin firing. The crack of the 4-inch echoed along the deck. All eyes turned toward the E-boat but the success of the night before was not to be repeated. Shells were seen to explode in the sea alongside the fast moving craft. The lean grey shape shrugged off the water cascading on her decks from the splashes and circled for another attack.

The next foray was different in nature as the Italian commander decided on a more cautious approach. The Oerlikon strikes had come as a nasty shock to Sot-totenente Fulgoni and he manoeuvred his command so as to attack from a greater distance. He ordered the quick-firer to concentrate on the bridge armament of his target. The makeshift gun's crew lined up the sights and began shelling. The initial salvo flew wastefully high but at the end of the run two direct hits were registered. The structure supporting the British gun was demolished, the weapon itself hanging down at a limp angle.

David cried out in shock as he felt the shells strike home beneath him. The two gunners were flung to one side by the impact. The circular gun pit was wrecked and one gunner, a broken arm flapping uselessly at his side, desperately wrestled his unconscious mate to safety with the other. A sailor appeared and began to assist the injured men.

"What the hell are you doing on my bridge?"

David turned to find Captain Pilgrim glowering at him.

Appalled at the violence of the previous few minutes, David could not find words to reply and simply raised the tool bag by way of explanation. It was left to Orme to clarify their mission.

"The steering telemotor, sir," he spluttered. "It's leaking—we came to fix it and top up the system."

"It takes two of you to repair a dribble?" scoffed Pilgrim. "Well, you can't do anything with that damned E-boat out there. Just stay out of my way."

David had the distinct feeling that the Captain's verbal assault was brought about more by the perilous situation than the presence of two boiler-suited engineers. The man's face was very pale and tense as he moved nervously about the bridge, keeping close to the safety of the steel bulkheads.

The E-boat raced in once more, its bow raised on a "V" of foaming seawater. The machine guns opened up once more; lazy lines of tracer accelerated into their target. Abruptly the port telegraph repeater erupted in a shower of shattered glass and twisted brass. David ducked futilely as a severed handle flew past his shoulder and smashed into a flag locker. As the attacker turned slightly the stern mounted quick-firer started pumping shells at *Arthurian Castle* but this time the gunners' aim was poor and no serious damage was done. There was a collective sigh of relief as the torpedo boat sheared off. They prepared for the next assault but Mas. 761 had broken off the engagement and was to be seen heading due north away from them.

"Ha! See that we've beaten them off, the cowards!" exclaimed Captain Pilgrim, pointing rather theatrically at the departing torpedo boat.

There was a silence on the bridge. The high tension of a moment before was replaced by relief tempered by a measure of embarrassment. Steve Orme looked at David, frowning.

"Let's have a look at this telemotor whilst we've got the opportunity," said David, shrugging. His apparent indifference concealed a certain disquietude; he'd watched Pilgrim's face as the Captain realised that they had survived. The relief was palpable and immense yet somehow worrying. The change of expression seemed to David to be akin to that which a condemned man must feel if spared the hangman's noose. Watson found his confidence in the man in command of the ship waning.

The two engineers placed their tools by the steering wheel. The wheel was set on a plinth that housed the controls that translated helm movements into hydraulic signals. Two small-bore pipes ran from the bridge to the steering flat where the transmitted pressures were used to regulate the steering engine and thence the massive rudder. A tiny amount of oil had leaked from the plinth, suggesting some damage, and it was this fault that they were to investigate.

"Let's get the covers off, Steve," said David.

They unbolted two large cast iron cover plates to expose the interior mechanism; immediately hydraulic oil flowed freely onto the wooden deck.

"Looks like more than a leaky joint," observed Orme.

"Aye, I'm surprised the steering is still working with this much leakage," David replied as he probed around the heavy iron casting. "Uh, huh! Here it is."

His fingers found a small perforation apparently caused by a stray bullet.

"The casting's got a hole in it and a lump of iron has broken off inside. It's jammed against the pipe. Probably nicked it; we'll need to put a clip around it for the time being."

They worked away carefully to make the repair over the next twenty minutes. Eventually David was satisfied with their joint efforts and they replaced the covers. As he stood up he noticed a mark on the plinth; it was a groove that he quickly deduced had been caused by another bullet. He traced its path to the point of impact on the compass pedestal. It took little further investigation to notice the twisted support for the all-important magnetic compass: their only means of steering a predetermined course. The damage was actually surprisingly slight, the bullet having expended most of its tremendous energy before contact. David examined the compass carefully. It seemed to be functioning satisfactorily even though he could see that it was leaning at a slight angle. He waved to the Third Officer.

"I may be wrong, but we may have a problem." He pointed at the damaged instrument, his finger tracing the effects of the bullet.

Colin Beck bent down to look, favouring his injured arm in its sling. He squinted awkwardly at the weakness David was indicating.

"I see what your getting at…" he replied doubtfully. "Any trouble with the compass?" He looked quizzically at the helmsman standing behind the steering wheel and taking frequent glances at the compass in its binnacle.

"Moves okay as the ship's head varies, sir; might be a bit slow though, come to think of it."

Beck grunted, then stood up nodding wryly at David. He moved over to where Pilgrim was standing and spoke quietly.

"What!" shouted the Captain. "Not the compass, surely. Show me."

David and his companion, still seated at the pedestal, squirmed out of the way. Pilgrim's face was bright red with anger and David had no wish for a confrontation with the man. The two engineers were totally ignored as the two deck officers examined the navigational aid.

As quickly as it had arisen, George Pilgrim's fury subsided to be replaced by an appearance of hopelessness as he accepted the uncertainty surrounding the accuracy of the compass. David was astonished by the sudden changes of emotion.

"Come on, Steve, let's get out of here. We've done our bit."

As they left the bridge they could see Pilgrim and Beck bent over the chart-table discussing the ship's position.

"Probably haven't been able to get a reliable sun-sight, what with all the attention we've been getting from the Italian Navy," said David as they dived down the companionway stairs.

"What? You mean they don't know where we are?" Orme looked shocked.

David grinned. "Of course they do! We're in the Med somewhere near Malta or maybe even Sicily!"

"Huh, very funny!"

The conversation was interrupted by the sudden shrilling of the alarms throughout the accommodation. As it happened, Sottotenente Fulgoni had not quite finished with *Arthurian Castle*. He had been forced to break off the engagement by his desperate shortage of fuel. However, on his slow economic speed passage back to base a reconnaisance aircraft, a seaplane under orders to find any convoy stragglers, had overflown him. A message was passed using the signalling lamp and before long two Savoia Marchetti 79 bombers were homing in on the reported position of the damaged merchantman. An early sighting of these marauders had prompted the initiation of the warning bells.

CHAPTER 15

▼

It was really a very simple attack. One aircraft came in from ahead whilst his partner swept in from the beam. *Arthurian Castle*'s gunners were forced to divide their attentions thus reducing the volume of fire directed at individual bombers. The two were separated by no more than twenty yards as they flashed over their quarry. Bombs screamed down on the unfortunate ship from different trajectories. The first explosions were in the water close alongside: three near misses but thankfully for the defenders no serious damage was sustained. There were other close shaves along the opposite flank of the merchantman but the centre missile of the stick vanished into the still open No. 4 cargo hatch. It exploded with a deep-throated roar and immediately obscured the entire vessel in a swirling cloud of flour dust.

A bomb dropped from abeam struck the deck in way of No.2 hold. The steel plating, already weakened in the earlier air raid, gave way and the projectile penetrated the cargo space. Its momentum scarcely diminished, it crashed into the ship's side, eventually emerging and exploding relatively harmlessly in the water alongside.

It was the last bomb of the side attack that proved to be the most lethal. It smashed its way through the side plating like a nail through a tire, reaching into the boiler-room. By the worst of bad luck it was deflected slightly in its path and eventually struck the vertical bulkhead separating the space from the adjacent engineroom. The resultant detonation could hardly have been more deadly. The bulkhead had a huge ten-foot wide hole ripped in it and steel fragments flew through the air like so many threshing scythes hacking into any hindrance to their passage. Unfortunately the unfettered release of the bomb's massive energy was also directed at the port boiler. The riveted Scotch boiler, already loaded internally with steam and water at 200 pounds per square inch pressure, was fractured. It erupted in a cataclysmic outpouring of scalding steam; the fifteen tons of water it contained flashed off into steam and a horrendous cloud blasted through the boiler-room and into the machinery space. The fireman, totally unaware of what was happening, died horribly, his spirit ripped from a body that was no match for the excessive temperatures.

The gushing shrieking high-pressure steam, rapidly expending its colossal energy, flooded the engine-room, striking down all in its path. The Second Engineer and his assistant together with the greasers all died abrupt painful deaths; scalded externally and with lungs seared, they could neither move nor breath as they slipped into darkness.

The huge release of pressure from the stricken boiler and the numerous fractured pipes left the main engine starved of steam. It gradually slowed and stopped, enveloped in a slowly condensing cloud. The noise of escaping steam subsided gradually and the ancillary machinery also ground slowly to a halt. *Arthurian Castle* drifted powerless and at the mercy of the attackers.

The two aircraft circled the motionless ship, their pilots trying to see through the enveloping clouds of flour dust what the results their assault had achieved. Finally one Savoia Marchetti pitched over in a shallow dive and released his last two missiles aimed at the centre of the cloud. Grievously wounded as *Arthurian Castle* was, her bad luck continued as the last bomb struck the deckhouse on the stern, exploding instantly. The 4-inch gun and her crew received a withering hail of red-hot fragments with deadly effects. Fred Gates was the only survivor although he didn't feel particularly fortunate as he staggered along the deck clutching an arm that poured blood at every hesitant step.

The impact of the boiler-room bomb threw David off his feet, at the same time tripping Orme. They rolled down the last few steps of the staircase into the alleyway leading aft. The ear-numbing screech from below them was unbearable. David gestured violently toward the after deck and the two engineers scrambled along the narrow corridor, conscious of a rapid rise of temperature as steam assaulted the inner bulkhead. They emerged thankfully onto the deck as the final attack was delivered. In the swirling flour dust it was not possible to know with certainty what was happening; that they had been struck again was not in doubt but no damage was immediately visible. David blinked rapidly in the heavy atmosphere trying to decide what he should do; Orme dithered, looking at him expectantly. Then out of the powdered gloom reeled a ghost, a white apparition with a bright red arm. The figure collapsed as it reached them. David knelt down and turned the man over before he recognised his friend. Gates had fainted from shock and lay in an untidy huddle on the black painted deck.

Recovering from the surprise of Gates' unexpected arrival, David wrenched at the gunner's shirt to expose the wound. The flesh was ripped away just below the shoulder and the gaping hole oozed blood ominously. Quickly he tore the shirt away from the area, then shredded it to make a makeshift bandage. With Steve Orme's help he managed to bind the wound tightly. The material quickly flushed red as it absorbed blood, but it seemed the outrush had been at least partially stemmed.

"Give me a hand to carry him down to my cabin," grunted David as he lifted a limp uninjured arm and began to haul Gates into a sitting position. Between them they managed to move the unconscious form back into the accommodation and eventually laid him on the bunk in David's room.

"We had best leave him here and find out what's happening down below in the engine-room. He should be okay for a little while at least."

Orme nodded, happy to be guided by the other man. The ship had become very quiet as the normally all-pervading thump of machinery had disappeared. There was an eeriness about the gently rolling stationary merchant ship. The silence was broken by shouts but the words were from too great a distance to be intelligible. David pressed his hand against the steel that formed the inner bulkhead of the engine-room; he recoiled rapidly as he felt the residual heat and shook his hand ruefully.

"Lets try the boat deck…might be able to see what's what through the engine-room skylights!" He turned toward the internal staircase.

They scrambled up two flights, along another alleyway and emerged onto a sunlit deck alongside one of the lifeboats. Turning aft, they passed a number of ventilators, wide pipes standing up from the deck like inverted letter 'J's. The flour had by now largely dispersed but a new cloud had taken its place in the centre of the ship. The metal skylight covers were held vertically open by steel bars and from the apertures thus created gushed a roiling haze of steam. It rose unhindered into the warmth of the day before gradually condensing; already the surrounding deck was wet with running water. The bulky figure of the Chief Engineer joined them.

"We'll wait for the steam to subside before trying to get into the engineroom," he said calmly. "It doesn't look good."

They were joined by the Chief Officer, Brian Crawshaw.

"What do you think, Chiefie?" he asked.

"We'll have to wait a while for the engineroom to cool down; then we'll be able to assess the damage."

The Mate nodded. "Right. I'll get off around the deck see what other damage we've got. At least the Italian Air Force has left us alone for the time being."

He pointed at two diminishing dots high in the sky. All four men stood watching the departing Savoia Marchetti's when abruptly there came from forward of the bridge a tremendous whoosh as a sheet of flame leapt from the wrecked No.2 hold. Unseen by anyone on board, a fire had been smouldering in the medical supplies that comprised the top layer of cargo. It had been caused by splinters from the original bomb that had struck the ship. In the confined space there had been insufficient air to sustain full combustion and the fire's progress had been slow. The second missile, even without exploding, had changed all that. By smashing it's way through deck and side it had opened an airway that fanned the smouldering wound dressings and medicines into flame. A case of medical alcohol bottles exploded in the heat and suddenly the conflagration roared out of control with flames licking hungrily as high as the bridge.

The quartet at the skylight stood rooted to the spot by the shock of the sudden fire, each in his own way trying to come to terms with this latest disaster. The hesitation lasted only seconds before Crawshaw began to speak. His words were immediately lost in a further ringing of alarms. There was a pattern to the tones.

Crawshaw swore vividly, "What the hell is he doing, sounding the Abandon Ship signal?"

He spun on his heel and charged off toward the bridge ladder.

"I guess he was referring to the Captain," observed David. "What do we do next, Chief?"

"I'm afraid we have to follow the rules…muster at our boat station ready to abandon. Pity those damn bells are on the battery supply circuit; with the generators out of action they wouldn't have operated…" McKay shrugged, leaving the sentence hanging.

They helped releasing covers and securing ropes from the starboard lifeboat. It was then lowered slightly to a position where it could be boarded. David's mind drifted back to his earlier lifeboat experience and the brief moments with Megan. Not for the first time he wished fervently that she were safe and well. His brief reverie was interrupted by voices raised in disagreement on the bridge. Crawshaw was arguing vehemently with the Captain, but his words were wasted as Pilgrim shouted at the top of his lungs: "This ship has a fire in a hold loaded with petrol next to an unexploded bomb! It is my duty to save the lives of those on board! Kindly follow my orders and attend your lifeboat."

With that he rushed down the ladder and began ordering people into the starboard lifeboat. It was at this point that David suddenly remembered Gates alone in his cabin. Realising that only Orme and himself knew of Gates' presence, he turned and left the boat deck hastily. His disappearance was not noted by those concentrating on boarding. The list of names that should have been checked was ignored in the rush to launch. Orme had already followed McKay across the ship to his designated position by the port craft.

Once the lifeboat was filled, Pilgrim gave orders to lower away. It descended rapidly and safely to float alongside the battered steel hull of *Arthurian Castle*. The oars were shipped and as the rowers pulled strongly the wooden craft moved rapidly away. Pilgrim's wild-eyed expression relaxed somewhat as the gap between the two hulls widened.

Over on the other side of the ship things progressed with more organisation. The muster list was checked before boarding and everyone accounted for with due allowance being made for those known to have been killed. The port side of the ship had born the brunt of the torpedo boat's attack and there was some damage to the lifeboat; hasty plugs were manufactured from scraps of clothing and rammed home as the vessel was lowered into the sea. The Mate, Brian Crawshaw, allowed the boat to float still attached to its launching falls whilst the leakages were attended to. He automatically surveyed the steep steel sides ranging above him: there were a number of shell and splinter holes but as far as he could see all the damage extended above the waterline.

They cast off the rope falls and slowly rowed away from the stricken ship. From a distance *Arthurian Castle* was a sorry sight. Smoke poured from the holes in her foredeck in thick heavy clouds. There was no longer any flame, yet somehow the increasing volume of grey fumes seemed to indicate a worsening situation. The skeletal wreckage of the bow served only to make the survivors even happier to have left the ship.

Crawshaw was alone in regretting the hasty orders that had resulted in the abandonment. He gazed disconsolately out to sea, his earlier anger replaced by numbness. His heart had told him that they should have stayed aboard but his sense of duty had led him to leave.

Fraser McKay, sitting with Steve Orme, ignored the ship but thought of the men who had been in the engineroom when the last bomb had struck. Around him men sat in silence, each with his memory of happier times on *Arthurian Castle* shared with crewmates who would not be joining them on the next run ashore.

CHAPTER 16

▼

David Watson knew when he entered his cabin that he stood a good chance of being abandoned aboard the ship. Fred Gates would not be leaving the room for some time. His friend lay motionless, still unconscious with only a trifling movement of his chest to show that he was still alive. Gates' face was unnaturally pale, his wounded arm a bright smear of colour as the blood continued to seep through the makeshift bandage.

David stood looking down at the wiry figure, shaken by the deterioration in the man's condition in such a short space of time and at a loss as to what he should do for the best. He put his hand to Gates' brow; it felt cold and clammy. He guessed that his friend was suffering from the shock of the wounding but he had no medical training upon which to draw for any treatment.

"Well, Fred, I don't know what I'm doing but I'll do my best," he said to the recumbent form.

Initially he pulled a blanket from a cupboard underneath the bunk and tucked it neatly around the invalid. As he did so he caught a glimpse through the porthole of a lifeboat pulling away from the ship.

"Looks like it's just you and me, Fred," he observed out loud. "Seems they've left us to it!"

He went across to the other side of the accommodation where there was a spare cabin. At some earlier date the room he was in had been designated the ship's hospital, a rather grandiose title for a space that was only recognisable in its duty by having a large locker for the storage of medical supplies. The locker was padlocked but David remembered that the key was held by the Chief Steward. He marched along the alleyway to that worthy's abandoned cabin and found what he was looking for hanging on a board with others all identified by metal tags. As he returned to the hospital, the cold clamp of isolation gripped him. He shrugged it off with an effort and concentrated on the task in hand.

The medical supplies were neatly stacked on shelves and contained in boxes. David scanned the names printed neatly thereon but found little that he recognised. Eventually he settled for a bottle of iodine, a couple of rolls of bandage and some lint dressings. As he turned to leave the hospital his eye was drawn to a tiny item on a lower shelf; he paused, then decided to supplement his equipment.

Fred Gates' condition had not changed when David returned. He gently eased the injured arm from under the blanket and stripped off the scrap of cloth covering the wound. The livid gash continued to seep blood as he examined it. He felt revolted by the gory mess but he forced himself to consider the wound logically. He reasoned that if major blood vessels had been ruptured the blood loss would be much greater. As far as he could see the blood was seeping generally from the lacerated flesh. He decided to try pulling together the edges of the wound so as to help limit the bleeding. Using a pad of lint dipped in alcohol, he carefully cleaned the whole area, then applied liberal quantities of iodine. Gates stirred and moaned whilst David worked but did not recover consciousness. Taking a deep breath, David picked up the curved needle he had found on the medical locker shelf. It was already threaded with a length of catgut, which was how he had recognised its purpose. He swilled it in the iodine for a few seconds, then lifted it up to the wound.

"I hope I'm doing the right thing, Fred," he said quietly as he fought to control his nerves. "I don't know any fancy stitches but I've got to do something to stop the bleeding."

He pierced the slippery flesh and began the task, his brow furrowed in deep concentration. Settling for the minimum of stitching, he finished one area of the gash quickly, but then spent what seemed like an age devising a method of locking the final suture to avoid the flesh separating again. As he became more adept his efforts became neater and finally he was satisfied that he could do no more. He washed fresh blood away, then applied a lint pad liberally soaked in iodine. He completed the dressing with a firmly wrapped clean white bandage. He was heartened to see that the bandage did not immediately become soaked in blood.

"Let's hope that works," he said to the ashen-faced gunner as he tucked the arm back under the blanket.

David sat for a long time beside his friend in case there should be a change in his condition, but Gates remained unconscious, occasionally groaning, yet unmoving. Finally satisfied that the patient's condition had stabilised, Watson took off in search of food. A further visit to the Chief Steward's cabin produced the necessary keys and he was able to access the food stores. It was while he was investigating the various storerooms that it occurred to him that the temperature in the accommodation had dropped. He found an area of bulkhead that formed one of the boundaries of the engineroom. The painted steel felt just slightly warm to the touch. He smiled to himself, aware that the steam flooding the space had largely condensed.

He busied himself frying eggs and bacon before returning to his patient to eat the meal. Gates remained pale, his breathing shallow, but somehow David felt he was a little more comfortable. After the meal he took a stroll on deck in the hope of seeing the ship's lifeboats but the visibility had deteriorated as the first of a succession of rainsqualls swept down on the vessel. Suddenly huge drops of water began to fall, hitting the sun-heated decks in a rapidly increasing noisy splatter. A cloud of vapour rose initially, only to be beaten down by the violence of the shower. David ducked back inside a watertight door entry and watched the downpour. *Arthurian Castle* was now the centre of his world, the horizons defined by the wall of falling rain. Strangely, he felt comforted by this image despite an acceptance that he was undoubtedly stranded aboard a floating time bomb. It never occurred to him that he should have left in the Captain's lifeboat when the opportunity had presented itself. Some minutes later, with the rain still drenching the ship, he returned to his vigil in the chair alongside Gates.

It was in the early hours of the morning that David was awakened from a light slumber. He opened his eyes, confused by the lack of light in that instant of wakefulness. He sensed a movement from the bunk.

"It's okay, Fred, you're in my bed," he said by way of reassurance.

He received a grunt by way of reply.

"Hang on, there's a torch in my drawer."

The weak yellow circle of light reflected from a pair of half open eyes. They closed abruptly.

"Do you mind not shining that thing in my eyes!" The voice was low and very weak but clear.

"Welcome back," greeted David enthusiastically. "Thought you were going to sleep all day."

"Umm, 'ow about a drink then?"

David eased the gunner into a sitting position and helped him to cope with a tumbler of water. The effort exhausted Gates who subsided back onto the mattress gratefully.

"Hang on a bit," said David, "I'll see if I can find an oil lamp that's working—then we can see what we're doing."

He returned in minutes with a lit hurricane lantern that he managed to hang from the redundant electrical light fitting in the centre of the room. The smoky flame radiated an insipid light that lent an eerie air to the cabin. Gates' lips twisted in an attempt at a smile. To David's eyes the wounded man looked less haggard if still desperately weak.

"Hang on," he said, "I'll be back in a jiffy."

True to his word David returned shortly with a steaming plate of porridge.

"We're lucky the galley range is oil fired. Hot food is still possible."

He helped Gates sit up again and proffered spoonfuls of the cereal. The meal was a painful event for Fred but he managed to eat a little as David explained the lack of lighting and the sequence of events following the detonation of the bomb that had demolished the 4-inch gun. He avoided any mention of the abandonment of the ship. Finally Gates lay back and soon fell into a deep natural sleep. David curled up on the tiny couch and was soon in a similar state.

They woke late the following morning. Gates looked much better and David felt heartened. He visited the galley once more and brought food back to the cabin for breakfast. With his assistance Fred managed to eat a reasonable amount.

"Take a rest whilst I have a prowl around," David grinned as he gathered the dirty plates and left the cabin.

Some in-built reluctance stopped him from investigating the fire in No.2 hold; instead he headed for the machinery spaces. The engineroom door was now quite cool and he felt safe in opening it a little. The weak fragmented daylight filtering in through the open skylights illuminated the top of the main engine. Aside from an excess of water on the covers and dripping from steel stanchions there seemed little at fault. It was only as David descended along the ladders and walkways that he could see the huge gash in the boiler room bulkhead and the wrecked pipework in the vicinity. He reached the bottom platform and walked through into the boiler room. Ignoring the bundle of rags and overheated flesh that was all that remained of the fireman, he carefully surveyed the damage caused by the percussion of the bomb and the violent depressurising of the port boiler. The destruction was terminal as far as the one side of the space was concerned, but he noted that the vital isolating valve that could be used to enable one boiler to be used with the other shut down was still in place and apparently operable.

In the engine spaces a number of minor steam lines had disappeared altogether. David knew that some pumps would have to be regarded as inoperable.

The worst damage he found was associated with the main condenser; one of the large diameter cooling water pipes had been fractured by explosive shock. It leaked seawater through a crack. Fortunately the crack had not opened unduly although David could see a large amount of leakage water swishing about in the engineroom bilge. He hastened to close a valve and, after a while, the dribble of water ceased. After an hour he was fairly clear in his mind as to the state of the machinery plant. He reflected ruefully that it was a pity that only he and Fred remained on board. It should be possible to raise steam again but it would take more than two men, even if both were fully fit, to achieve this. He pulled a large roll of tarpaulin from the store and covered the sad remains of the Second Engineer and his watch mates before returning to his cabin.

Gates was awake and gazing ruminatively at the deckhead rivets.

"How's it feel then, Fred?" asked David.

"Fine, but 'ow come the ship's so quiet? Don't sound like there's anybody about." Gates sounded vaguely accusative.

David grimaced but decided to tell his friend the full story.

"There's only us two left on board. Captain Pilgrim ordered everyone to abandon ship…the lifeboats left yesterday afternoon almost twenty-four hours ago."

"They didn't wait for you?" asked Gates.

"I'm not sure that in the panic anyone checked that the ship was clear of people."

"So what do we do now?"

"To be honest I haven't a clue. Stay here and, if the ship doesn't blow up, the bombers will find us again. There's a liferaft we could use if you feel up to it but I haven't a clue as to where we are. It could be just as risky as staying put. A bit of out of the frying pan into the fire."

They discussed various options but without reaching a conclusion and eventually the conversation became more general.

"So what will you do after the war," asked David at one stage.

Fred grinned at the assumption that the two men would survive but made no direct comment. "I suppose I'll stay in the Andrew if'n they'll 'ave me. It's not a bad life once you get used to it."

"Yeah, I know what you mean," replied Watson. "There's no way I could go back to the shipyards again after having come away to sea."

"That's it, no going back to a dead-end job wi' no prospects," declared Fred feelingly. "I'm only a gunner but I'm young, I've got experience now and I reckon if I worked at it I could get to be a petty officer."

"Have you got a girl friend, Fred?" asked David in an abrupt change of subject.

Gates looked slightly startled yet replied sheepishly, "No-one particular. Like to play the field, me! I take it you 'ave though, eh?"

"That's the problem, really. I met someone I'd like to have as my girl but, well, she's a bit posh. I can't see us having a future and anyway I'm not sure if she's still alive."

He went on to explain about Megan, her presence during the sinking of *Petrain Castle* and the lifeboats setting sail for Africa as he was taken aboard the U-boat.

Fred whistled. "The boss's daughter, eh! I see what you mean about posh."

David nodded glumly.

"Mind you, things'll be different after the war. You mark my words! Maybe shipowner's daughters and ship's engineers will be able to get together," offered Fred firmly.

David smiled. "Maybe!" He was silent for a moment staring abstractly into space. "You know what, Fred, I think you could be right. One thing's for sure, I'm going to give it a go."

"We'd best find a way back to Blighty then, Wattie. The sooner the better, eh what?"

The occupants of the port lifeboat shared a frugal meal and a few sips of water. Crawshaw had instigated a strict rationing regime from the outset. He guessed they could be floating around for some little while before being rescued and at that the likelihood was that any rescuer would be an enemy. There was precious little food aboard the wooden craft and only two small drums of fresh water. A rainsquall during the morning had enabled everyone to drink their fill catching something of the downpour in any receptacle that came to hand. Crawshaw idly wondered if, say, the Chief Engineer would have drunk water from his hat if he were still aboard *Arthurian Castle*.

They had drifted through the night but in the new day Crawshaw had organised parties of rowers and set a southerly course. The boat was equipped with neither sails nor a compass and the Mate was obliged to use the sun to achieve a rudimentary mode of navigation. He doubted that they had made much progress toward the Tunisian coast particularly as such wind as existed was from that direction.

In late afternoon, with improving visibility, they were heartened to see, in the distance, a medium sized merchant ship apparently heading away from them.

"What do you think, Chief?" he looked across at Fraser McKay, his eyebrows raised questioningly.

"Difficult to tell at this distance but she must be a straggler from the convoy. I'm not sure she's moving, you know."

"I thought she might be drifting too but I can't see any obvious damage."

It became quite clear that the strange vessel was indeed stationary and Crawshaw steered toward it as the rowers pulled strongly. It was a long hard pull, complicated by the odd rainsquall that occasionally obscured vision. Gradually they overhauled the freighter.

"She looks to be down by the head a bit," observed McKay.

"Aye that stern's sticking up quite a bit; probably why she's stopped," replied Crawshaw.

The ship remained stubbornly headed away from them such that it was impossible to make out details. The drab grey paintwork was similar to any of the cargo vessels in the convoy as was the stern mounted gun. The unknown vessel drifted from view once more as another shower passed between the two craft. Crawshaw altered course a fraction, encouraging his tiring rowers to continue their efforts.

"Looks like the gun took a bit of a pasting," he said, pointing past the Chief Engineer.

At this distance it was noticeable that the gun barrel was pointing an odd angle, but what was more significant was the view along the side as they closed at a slightly wider angle. Where the lifeboat should have been stowed on the starboard side was a gap overlooking two unattached sets of fall ropes.

"Looks like she may be abandoned. Pity they painted the names out under the wartime regulations…I'd love to know what ship she is," said McKay.

Crawshaw smiled broadly as he examined the vessel. "Yes, it might be very interesting to know her name."

McKay looked at him oddly, then back at the freighter. "You don't mean…?"

The Mate nodded. "Welcome home to good old *Arthurian Castle*."

"But how come she's ahead of us?"

Crawshaw shrugged. "Some odd quirk of the current, helpful wind…could be anything, I don't know."

As they closed the ship everyone began to notice odd things about her that they claimed to recognise. There was an excited buzz of conversation around the lifeboat as Crawshaw brought them neatly alongside. Willing hands grappled for the dangling falls and secured the little craft.

"Notice anything different about her, Chief?"

McKay looked puzzled as he gazed upwards along the broad shell damaged expanse of the freighter's side. He shook his head in bafflement as he turned back to face Crawshaw.

The Mate pointed at the sky above the bow. "No smoke from No.2 hold!"

CHAPTER 17

▼

The truck ride had been very uncomfortable. With the only seats occupied by armed soldiers, Megan and her two companions had been forced to sit on the floor. The first part of their journey along a narrow rutted track through dense jungle had strained the vehicle's suspension to the limit and had imparted fierce bone-jarring thumps to their rapidly tiring bodies. Later they had joined a met-alled road that, despite being in a poor state of repair, had made their progress slightly more bearable. There had been very little conversation mainly due to the sheer racket inside the canvas covering the rear of the truck. The exhaust silencer had disappeared long before and the resultant roar assaulted the senses unceas-ingly. Eventually they had arrived at a small town where the survivors had disem-barked.

Now, two days later, Megan was beginning to feel isolated. Rafferty and Edwards had been taken off to the local jail while she had been installed in a delightful old French colonial mansion that had been converted into a hotel for the benefit of the Vichy-French Governmental staff. As LeBrun had explained, "The prison is not equipped for the comfort of a lady." Megan had to admit that her room was very satisfactory: a clean airy space with broad full-length windows that opened out onto a tiny veranda that afforded her a panoramic view of the whole port area. She lay on the single bed staring at the ceiling, bored and frus-trated by the forced inactivity. As far as she was concerned it appeared that "internment" meant an extended stay in an acceptable hotel. LeBrun had made no comments regarding the future and she was forced to conclude that he expected her to sit out the war enjoying the West African climate. The prospect dismayed Megan, a young lady used to an active productive existence. She wondered idly how Rafferty and Edwards were taking to life in the jail. There appeared to be no restriction on her movement both within and without the hotel; indeed LeBrun had largely left her to her own devices, presumably because in the sea port of Grand-Bassam there was no means of escape. A single soldier stood guard outside the building and he accompanied her whenever she took a stroll.

A brief sortie around the immediate environs of the hotel had shown that it had been built on a long finger of land stretching eastward along the coast. On one side she could see the long rollers of the Atlantic Ocean whilst on the other the smooth waters of a large lagoon provided welcome shelter for a varied collection of boats. She had recognised two ocean-going schooners anchored in front of a mass of smaller craft that might have been the local fishing fleet, but of more interest had been the extensive wharves along the inner shoreline. Judging by the size of the mooring bitts secured at intervals to these structures, Megan had deduced that deep-sea cargo ships must visit the port from time to time.

Impulsively she rose from the bed, left the room and went down a wide staircase to the hotel foyer. She sauntered through the front door and into the bright afternoon sunlight. She smiled at the soldier sweating in the heat. "Come on, Pluto," she said, aware that he knew no English and could not therefore be insulted by the epithet. He followed at a distance with a shambling gait and the downcast expression that had led her to give him the nickname. There were only two main streets in that area of the town running along the length of the finger of land. Megan strode along the innermost, reaching an intersection. She turned, walked on and soon reached the second paralleling the beach. The Mairie, a fine two story building with white pillars framing an imposing arched doorway, was the place where, she believed, LeBrun had his office. Confidently stepping up a short stairway, she entered the establishment.

A broad reception area was flanked by a series of doors but directly in front of her stood a heavy mahogany desk. She strode up to it and peered over at a young African girl seated on the other side.

"Monsieur LeBrun?"

The girl stood up smiling; she offered some words in French but her accent was so thick that Megan could not understand. She remained at the desk shaking her head. The receptionist walked past, beckoning. Megan followed and was eventually shown into a wide office. LeBrun was seated at a desk poring over some papers on the pad in front of him. He extended his hand in the direction of a seat.

"Welcome, Mademoiselle Baxendell, please have a seat. Would you care for a drink? A coffee, perhaps? Or something cool?" LeBrun positively gushed as he welcomed his guest. Megan had the impression that he was pleased to see her if only as a distraction to a humdrum working day.

"Thank you, no," she declined graciously.

"Then what can I do for you?"

Megan took a deep breath, determined to make her point firmly. "Why are my friends being kept in a jail? They're not criminals!" She glared at LeBrun, meeting his eye until he was forced to look away. He cleared his throat but before he could speak she attacked again. "They are internees and deserve to be treated better than common thieves. I demand they be released immediately." She sat back expectantly.

"But, Mademoiselle, please! Where else can they stay? I cannot have them escaping."

"Escaping!" Megan exploded. "Escaping? And just where would they escape to? These are British Merchant seamen who've survived torpedoing by a cowardly German submarine. They are not from the Royal Navy who could at least have defended themselves. They're non-combatants, for goodness sake!"

LeBrun held his hands up in a gesture of defeat, cutting off Megan in full flow.

"I will look into," he replied in a strangled voice.

Megan clung to her advantage. "I should think so, indeed, and whilst you're about it please arrange for me to visit the jail to see my friends!"

"But of course," replied the Frenchman resignedly. He went on to explain where the prison was located. The rest of the interview consisted of LeBrun desperately trying to get Megan to leave his office without any further loss of dignity whilst she endeavoured to reinforce her point. She eventually decided that she had gone as far as she could that day and rose to leave. As she opened the office door she spun round and added a parting shot, "I'll be back tomorrow to see what arrangements you've made. Now I'm off to the jail, *Mister* LeBrun." She flounced out, leaving the Frenchman dumbfounded.

The short walk to the prison took just minutes with the little soldier floundering in her dusty wake. She banged on an exterior door and waited impatiently. There was the sound of locks being turned and then she could see into the courtyard of the establishment. An African warder led her to the Commandant's office. She stood in front of a desk staring at an elderly Frenchman dressed in an impeccable white uniform. He returned a telephone earpiece to its hook and stood up with an audible click of the heels.

"Mademoiselle Baxendell, *enchante*."

Megan mentally congratulated herself on at least a partial success: clearly LeBrun had advised the Commandant of her intended visit. Unfortunately her host spoke no English but he had obviously been ordered to allow her to meet with Rafferty and Edwards. He led her to a small room containing a table and four chairs; the other two survivors were already there drinking coffee from mugs. The Commandant chattered on in French but the words just flowed over her unheeded as she greeted the others. She felt greatly relieved to be with them once again, then, unbidden, came the thought that it would have been even better if David Watson could have been there also.

"We wondered where you'd been taken," began Rafferty.

Megan explained her situation in a few short sentences, in a hurry to get to the matter that was troubling her.

"We seem to be stuck here for the duration. LeBrun seems to have no plans to do other than provide board and lodging."

"There's not much we can do about that," Edwards spoke for the first time, "at least not banged up in here."

"Yes, I know," replied Megan, "but I've already put in a word for you with LeBrun."

She went on to outline her plans. As she finished speaking Rafferty whistled softly. "Wow!" he said feelingly. "Let's hope old LeBrun plays the white man and lets us out of here; then we might just have a chance."

As Megan left the prison compound she felt satisfied with her day's work. She returned to her hotel with renewed confidence, stepping out quickly and leaving "Pluto" struggling to keep up.

As it happened the two men were destined to remain incarcerated for a further week. The reasons were really only domestic although Megan refused to accept such a premise. She visited LeBrun every morning in order to demand action. The Frenchman for his part struggled to find somewhere that could be made available to house the Britishers. There was little if any accommodation suitable for visitors to Grand-Bassam and eventually he was reluctantly forced to move them to where Megan was living.

The three were reunited one evening and celebrated with some local beer that Edwards had managed to prise out of the hotel manager.

"All we need now is some transport," observed Megan as they broke up to return to their rooms for the night.

CHAPTER 18

▼

David Watson was amazed to hear the sound of voices coming from the deck. He dashed from his cabin and stopped abruptly as he nearly collided with the bulky figure of Fraser McKay.

"Well now, what are you doing still here, eh, Wattie?" said McKay in equal surprise.

"I was in my cabin…one of the gunners, Fred Gates, was injured." David shrugged his shoulders expressively. "I guess the lifeboats left without me!"

The Chief Engineer grinned. "Well, we came back, so think yourself lucky."

"But how did it happen?" asked David. "There was no sign of any boats when I was on deck this morning."

"We're not really sure. We spotted the ship and rowed for her without realising that she was the old *Arthurian*. Having caught up it seemed the thing to do to re-board, particularly as the fire in No.2 hold seems to be out," explained McKay.

Brian Crawshaw and a small party of sailors struggled with the tattered remains of the tarpaulin that had been stretched over the damage to the foredeck hold. The fire had scorched its way through in many places and the remnants proved awkward to tidy away. Finally, the canvas was removed and it was possible to appraise the devastation caused by bombs and fire. A clean hole through the starboard deck was matched by another in the side plating. It was possible to see the water gurgling around the ship just beneath the second aperture whilst standing on the deck. The wooden hatch covers were smashed and splintered in many places; some of the holes were blackened around the edges as evidence of the fire that had flared so suddenly. The steel of the surrounding deck was pitted and scarred with many small perforations from flying bomb fragments. The most serious damage was at the forward port corner of the hatch coaming. A large portion of the steel structure had disappeared and a five-foot wide hole gaped obscenely. Crawshaw bent over the breach inspecting what he could see of the cargo.

No.2 hold had been filled on the Clyde with aviation spirit and medical supplies; the heavy petrol drums were in the lower part of the hold and covered by a wide hatch fitted with wooden covers. By good fortune the burning dressings, drugs and equipment had not consumed these covers in the brief violent conflagration. The flames, fanned by air rushing through the gash in the side, had burned their way upwards through the readily combustible supplies, but once this material had been engulfed the fire had declined naturally. In a way the very inflammability of the medicines had helped the survival of *Arthurian Castle*: the fire had come and gone so quickly that it had not got a hold on the vulnerable lower hatch covers. The fuel for the Malta Spitfires had not been overheated and the possibility of a ship-destroying explosion had been avoided.

All of this became clear to Crawshaw as he continued his inspection; he accepted that luck had played a big part in the ship's continued survival.

"Lets get these burnt hatch covers off: we need to make sure that the fire is out!" he shouted across to the Bosun. The sailors got to work as he strode down the deck past the accommodation block and along the after deck. The damage here was not so bad, he decided; the open hold with its demolished flour cargo showed something of the force of the exploding bomb, even allowing for much of the impact having been absorbed in the soft sacks. The small aftermost deckhouse, hit by a further missile, was almost totally demolished. He walked around the contorted metal in order to check the 4-inch gun mounting. A quick glance identified a twisted barrel and a heavily gouged breechblock; he made a mental note to have the bloodied remains of the unfortunate gun crew removed for burial as he retraced his steps forward.

A little later he met up with Fraser McKay who had just finished a tour of the engineroom with David Watson.

"What do you think then, Chief?"

"Umm, David had had a good look around earlier on and things are a bit of a mess, but with a little luck we should be able to get under way again. It would be only half speed or so—one boiler's totally done for—but we can give it a go. What about your side of the house?"

"It looks like the fire is out but the hull is punctured in a lot of places. Nothing too serious taken in isolation but as a whole I'll not be happy until we've plugged those we can get at. The thing that does worry me is the bow down attitude we noticed from the lifeboat. It's not much at the moment but I'm not sure what's causing it yet. If the collision bulkhead is cracked after that torpedo hit us it may be that No.1 hold is flooding. I'll get the Bosun to check the hold bilges for water and I may need a pump to empty them."

McKay nodded in acceptance. "That should be okay once we get steam up again. Look, why don't we compare notes again in, say, four hours? It's going to take at least that long to sort out down below?"

Crawshaw clapped his colleague on the shoulder by way of encouragement. "I'll be on the bridge if you need me."

In the engineroom David and Steve Orme were attempting to fire up the starboard boiler. With the death of the Second Engineer and his assistant, they were the only other engineers left on board since the Third and his mate had joined the Captain's lifeboat. The hand fuel pump, used to start a cold boiler, was fitted on the port side of the boiler-room and had suffered in the bombing as a result. It was irreparable and the only way to raise steam was to fill one of the furnaces with wood and light it. That way it was hoped to be able to power the steam driven fuel pump such that normal oil firing of the boiler could be resumed.

A huge pile of timber dominated the stokehold, a stoker taking pieces from it at intervals to feed into a gaping furnace. An orange-red ball of fire billowed in the broad corrugated iron tube; baulks of timber crackled and spat as they crumbled to ash. A draught of air rushing through pulled smoke and sparks into the funnel uptakes.

David peered anxiously at the steam pressure gauge but it remained stubbornly at zero. He looked at the dwindling pile of lumber trying to make an impossible calculation. There were parties of men scouring the ship for any further supplies but he was beginning to think that it was going to be touch and go as to whether they would have sufficient for the task in hand.

As if reading his mind Orme spoke up, "This could be interesting! Do you think the Mate will mind if we start burning the cabin furniture?"

"It might well come to that, you know," replied David, taking his colleague's slightly flippant remark seriously. "This ship isn't going anywhere without steam and we can't raise steam any other way."

"Ooo, good," laughed Orme. "Shall I tell the lads to start stripping the Captain's stateroom? They'll like that!"

David did not reply as at last the pressure gauge began to register. Another plank was thrown into the maw of the furnace to be rapidly consumed, but once the pressure began to rise it continued; soon there was 50 pounds per square inch showing.

"What do you think? Will the fuel pump run at such a low pressure?" The question was rhetorical, as David had already decided to try. He gave instructions to Orme who vanished up the steel-runged ladders to open stop valves on the top of the boiler. Soon there was a bubbling of water from the pump drains shortly followed by a low gushing of leaking steam. David allowed the pump to warm up as the remainder of the wood was thrust into the furnace fire. He opened the steam valve, closed the drain and the machine wheezed into life. He glanced suspiciously at the boiler pressure gauge but it had not dropped appreciably. As the pump clanked up and down a few times he knew they were going to get away with it: within half an hour the boiler was re-established with oil fuel firing its three furnaces.

Orme rejoined him. "There's quite a few leaks up there," he said, nodding upwards.

"Let's hope they take up as the pipes warm through," replied David hopefully.

Luck was not with them, however, and it turned out to be a long night for the two engineers. As they circulated steam to the essential machinery more damage was discovered. The impact of the bomb had fractured a number of lines and more than once they were obliged to shut down the boiler whilst they made temporary repairs. Fraser McKay joined them wearing a clean boiler suit that rapidly became begrimed and sodden with sweat. David looked at him at one stage and smiled; the Chief normally kept his overalls clean and unstained during his inspection tours of the engineroom. To have his superior looking as dirty and dishevelled as himself was a new experience. But the effort was necessary; it took all the energy and experience of the three men to get the machinery running again. Finally in the early hours of the morning they were ready to restart the main engine.

"We'll split the watches between the three of us," stated McKay as they warmed the big steam engine through. "I'll take the four to eight; you can decide between yourselves which watch you want. I'm off up to the bridge to let the Mate know we're ready to start."

Crawshaw gazed moodily through the bridge windows. It was a clear starry night with a light swell; the drifting cargo ship rolled ponderously to the turgid sea. Reports had shown that there was water in No.1 hold and he was mentally reviewing the situation. It was probable that the level would continue to rise even when the pumps were available again. This would force the bow deeper, thus increasing the speed of flooding: worse still, the bulkhead between No.1 and No.2 hold would come under increasing pressure both from the weight of water and also the effects of the ship's forward momentum. He sighed, aware that a difficult few days lay ahead with every chance that *Arthurian Castle* would founder before she gained the shelter of a Maltese harbour.

"Penny for them!" a voice carried through the gloom at his side. He turned, recognising the bulk if not the face of the man moving in alongside him.

"Hello there, Chief. When can we get under way again?"

"As soon as you like; the lads are standing by down below. We'll take it easy…see what we can get out of the remaining undamaged machinery, okay?"

The mate alerted the helmsman, then swung the brass handle of the surviving telegraph to 'Full Ahead'. Shortly there came a tremble through the fabric of the ship that slowly built to a low rumbling vibration. *Arthurian Castle* gathered way once more as the bow swung gracefully onto course.

"Before daybreak I'll try to get a star sight so that I can work out our exact position. We know that there is a question mark against the compass and, frankly, we could be anywhere. Meanwhile we'll head down toward the North African coast before turning east again. In the first place that will give me a chance to estimate how inaccurate the compass has become and in the second we'll put some distance between us and the enemy's bases on Sicily," explained Crawshaw.

"What about the minefields on the way into Malta?" asked McKay.

"Unfortunately the charts giving their positions appear to have been destroyed when Captain Pilgrim left the ship. I thought that if we made it to the Tunisian coast, then stayed just outside their territorial waters, we should be able to skirt at least part of the mined area." Crawshaw sounded less than confident but the big engineer made no comment.

Progress through the rest of the night and the new morning could best be described as sedate. The engine revolutions had been increased to 55 rpm but this figure had reduced significantly when the steam-driven General Service pump had been started in an effort to control the rise of water in No.1 hold. The Mate judged that they were making good just short of 5 knots in a southerly direction. The navigation compass, as far as he could judge from the position fix he'd managed to work out, was inaccurate by up to 10 degrees. He knew that the noon sight would enable him to plot a more reliable position and hence to estimate the compass error more precisely. At this stage of their solo voyage he was not too concerned with accurate navigation but he knew that the dash northward from the coastline toward Malta would be far more taxing; not that *Arthurian Castle* was likely to be doing much "dashing" given her wounds.

Crawshaw leaned over the chart once more familiarising himself with as much detail as possible. It was unfortunate that the large-scale plan, the one that delineated the minefields, was no longer available; it nagged at the edges of his consciousness that he might be missing something because it didn't show up on the only chart available to him. His tired brain was taking longer and longer to deal with information and he knew that he must find time to sleep before the final critical stages of the passage. Being the only navigating officer still on the ship, he had no-one with whom to share the watchkeeping duties. He turned the matter over in his mind before accepting that the main requirement for keeping a look out would be to have foreknowledge of an impending enemy attack: the Bosun could fulfil that roll admirably, he decided. Thus it was that when the reconnaissance aircraft, a Cant seaplane, found them just before dark, Brian Crawshaw was sleeping on a makeshift bed in the chart room.

He stumbled back onto the bridge blinking eyes that felt as if they had been covered with sandpaper lids, desperately trying to focus on the tiny spot that was being pointed out to him. He cursed inwardly; although there was nothing he could have done to avoid the ship being sighted, some part of him felt guilty at being asleep when the Italian aeroplane arrived. He studied their aerial shadow as the last vestiges of sleep left him. Suddenly he turned and swung the telegraph lever violently to the "Dead Slow" position. A slight smile touched his lips as the engine vibration diminished noticeably. At least they're still awake down below, he thought, as he returned to his perusal of the Cant.

"They'll be trying to estimate our speed of advance," he explained to the hovering Bosun. "It's too late for them to mount an air strike this evening. If we slow down a bit it might throw them off a wee bit."

He strode over to the engineroom telephone and cranked the handle. "Hello, who's that? Ah, Chief, good. Look, we've been spotted…a seaplane. I've slowed down to give him the impression that we've sustained even more damage. Thing is, how much more speed can you give me when it leaves at nightfall?"

There was silence at the other end of the line for a moment before the tinny voice responded, "We can mebbe squeeze a touch more out of the boiler, but the biggest gain would come if we could shut the G.S. pump down for a while. It gobbles the steam, you know."

It was a conundrum: whether to opt for maximum speed with the chance of dodging the enemy but risking a catastrophic increase in the water level in No.1 hold, or to continue at their earlier speed with the enhanced risk of being attacked again.

To his credit Crawshaw did not hesitate. "I understand, Chief. We'll continue at this speed whilst we're being observed; then we'll shut off the pump and go for every revolution you can manage. In the meantime, if you can increase the pumping rate, please do so."

Hanging up, Crawshaw wondered if he was doing the best for his shipmates. He mulled over his problem for only a short while before he noticed the seaplane shearing off toward the north, clearly intent in reaching its base before nightfall. As it disappeared he pushed the telegraph back to "Full Ahead" before using the telephone once more.

"That's it, Chief! I'm going to alter course slightly. You can shut the pump down now." Without waiting for a reply he hung up the receiver and turned to give the helmsman new course orders.

The bow swung slightly in the gathering gloom and he was gratified to feel an increased urgency in the engine vibration rattling loose fittings on the bridge. *Arthurian Castle* plodded on through the hours of darkness gradually building up to a speed of over 6 knots. Her course diverged appreciably from that which she had been following when spotted by the Italian aircraft. It was clear on the bridge as a new day dawned that they were well away from any projected position that the enemy might investigate. Of course, a determined search would inevitably lead to the ship being found but Crawshaw was hoping that the Italians would not spend too long looking for a single damaged merchantman still a long way from Malta. Unfortunately the safety inherent in avoiding detection had been achieved at a heavy price. The water level had continued to rise in the foremost hold, but worse still the rate of ingress was accelerating as the ship's bow drooped ever lower in the sea.

At daybreak they reverted to the slower speed with pumps once more working to control the leakage in No.1 hold. The weather remained clear throughout the day and lookouts increased their vigilance, aware that the ship would be visible over a considerable distance. It was a day of extreme tension for all onboard expecting the Italian and German Air Forces to appear above them like the sword of Damocles. Indeed, so concerned were the skeleton crew aboard *Arthurian Castle* about what might be awaiting them in the skies that the inboard potential for disaster, the unexploded bomb, was temporarily quite forgotten.

CHAPTER 19

▼

The little West African port of Grand-Bassam seemed to wake from its slumbers as the small freighter eased its way into its berth and tied up. Workers appeared as if by magic and soon the hatches were opened and cargo began to be discharged. There was little urgency about the operation, yet paradoxically its very smoothness saw a rapid movement of her load. For the three British internees the steamer was a welcome sight indeed. Rafferty dubbed the ship in a moment of hopeful if plagiaristic eloquence, *The Road to the Isles*. The trio had discussed plans for escape at great length once they were reunited at Megan's hotel but the main stumbling block to any hope of implementation had always been a means of transportation. The local steamer represented a possible escape route and they were united in their determination to make every effort to stowaway when she left the port.

By way of preparation they had taken to making a regular stroll along the commercial quays that lined the lagoon each afternoon. There had of course been nothing to see of particular interest before the arrival of the ship but Pluto, their faithful soldier/escort, had become used to the daily ritual. He was not unduly perturbed, therefore, when they strolled past the moored vessel as it continued to be unloaded.

"There seems to be only the one access gangway," said Megan.

"Yes, that would be normal," replied Rafferty, "you'll probably find there's someone at the head of the gangway detailed to stop anyone boarding unnoticed."

"So there's no easy way aboard," observed Megan in a voice tinged with disappointment.

They continued past the steamer without stopping and trying to show only a minimal interest in the activity surrounding the vessel. It was possible to make out a name painted at the bow; the rust streaked, flaking letters announced *Shivandra* to the world. There were two holds set into a well deck just forward of a lumpy accommodation block that was itself surmounted by a spindly funnel. The ship had clearly seen better days, the amount of rust exceeding the painted areas noticeably. Some of the plating of her hull was heavily scarred and looked to Dick Rafferty's professional eye to be in a state of terminal corrosion. Yet he had to admit that despite the apparent lack of maintenance, the derricks and associated equipment seemed to be operating smoothly as a large cargo net full of bulging sacks was swung ashore. He glanced up at the bridge and locked eyes with a white shirted figure leaning comfortably on the rail. Rafferty nodded amiably but the face remained emotionless as the dark eyes continued to bore into his own. He looked away hurriedly, unsettled by the stare.

The little procession turned into a street leading away from the cargo quay and soon the freighter was lost to view.

"Let's stop for a coffee," said Megan as they walked along the dusty streets. She mimed drinking from a cup, smiling and nodding for the benefit of Pluto who, understanding her intention, beamed and ducked his head enthusiastically. They stopped at a tiny bistro and were soon savouring the locally grown coffee, freshly ground to their order. Megan paid with French francs. She had managed to convert the few English pounds Rafferty had carried in his wallet at an exorbitant rate in the hotel. It came as something of a surprise that English currency would be acceptable until she remembered that some of the surrounding states would be sympathetic to the British cause and therefore sterling would be exchangeable generally within the West African communities.

"Perhaps we could slip aboard at night," proposed Edwards as he relaxed over the strong black brew.

Rafferty recalled the face that had scrutinised him and felt a wave of doubt yet he nodded at Edwards. "Probably our best option."

"But won't the sentry or whatever he is still be by the gangway?" asked Megan.

"I think any gangway is probably out whatever the time of day. To start with, those things tend to rattle against the ship's side. The chances of sneaking aboard unheard would be pretty slim." Rafferty spoke slowly but thoughtfully.

Megan opened her mouth to speak but stopped as she saw the concentration furrowing the young man's forehead. There was silence as they finished their drinks. Pluto, sitting at an adjacent table, gazed curiously across at them.

"How do you fancy shinning along the mooring ropes, Megan?" said Rafferty at length.

"I'm not much good at that sort of thing I'm afraid," she replied.

Rafferty nodded absently. "I wonder what cargo she's going to be loading? It might be possible to hide you in amongst packing cases or some such. What do you think, Edwards?"

"Worth a try, sir," the erstwhile greaser replied enthusiastically. Megan grimaced but said nothing, waiting for Rafferty's further thoughts but there were none. Instead, Dick stood and, beckoning the others, started back toward the hotel. Megan felt disappointed but trudged along silently with her companions. The evening meal was a restrained affair with conversation limited to speculation as to the destination of *Shivandra*. The hope was that she would voyage to another African port where feeling would be more pro-British and internment less likely. Certainly the consensus view was that they would have a greater chance of repatriation to England if they could get away from the Vichy French dominated Ivory Coast.

Dick Rafferty slipped away to his room after the meal with a mumbled excuse about having a headache. He moved a chair up to the window and stared out moodily; as the darkness provided a curtain at the end of another hot day he continued his vigil. After only a few minutes he was rewarded with a stirring of movement on the steps leading up to the front door of the hotel. Pluto had decided that his period of duty was over and he slowly moved off away from the dim illumination spilling out from the hotel's doors and windows. From previous observation Rafferty knew that the soldier would not be replaced. He wondered idly whether that was because there was no-one else available to take his place or whether the powers that be assumed that the internees would be unlikely to leave their quarters after nightfall. Whatever the reasoning it was faulty, he decided as he quietly slipped out of his room. Avoiding the well-lit foyer, he passed along a corridor leading to a rear entrance that he negotiated without being observed.

The thoroughfares of Grand-Bassam were not provided with street lighting, but it was a clear night and the moonlight was sufficient for him to find his way. He strode quickly in the direction of the cargo quay and was soon standing in shadow by a warehouse scanning the ghostly bulk of *Shivandra*. Most of the ship was in darkness outlined against a starry sky, but an open door radiated brightly against the surrounding gloom. A figure obscured the emanating light briefly as a crewman passed through the opening carrying a bucket. He moved to the ship's side and there was a splash as he deposited the contents of the bucket in the lagoon.

Although Rafferty stood hidden watching the ship he saw no other activity over half an hour although occasional sounds of music carried to him on the fitful breeze. He decided to investigate the warehouse. It was an open fronted affair with tall broad doors that were closed tightly and locked. He moved around the side of the building, seeking a window that might have been left open. He drew a blank; the back of the construction was equally unhelpful and he was beginning to lose hope of making an entry when his questing fingers found a small doorway let into the end of the third wall. He seized the doorknob and was vaguely surprised to find it turn easily under his hand. He slipped inside without making a sound and closed the door behind himself. It was pitch black and he stood unmoving waiting for his heartbeat to slow down somewhat. Eventually he took a box of matches from his trouser pocket, struck one and peered around. He was in a small office equipped with a desk untidily bestrewn with paperwork and two straight-backed wooden chairs. As the match sputtered out he glimpsed an oil lamp hanging from the low ceiling. It was the work of seconds to lift it down and light the wick from a second match. An eerie orange pervaded the space, revealing a small window to one side of the door he had just come through. Fearing discovery, he moved quickly to another, internal, door which clearly led into the interior of the warehouse; once through this access he felt reasonably confident that the oil lamp would not be visible to anyone outside the building.

Rafferty spent a long time examining piles of goods ready for shipment. By far the largest stack was comprised of sacks of coffee beans all neatly stencilled with the name of the ship. There was also an amount of cocoa in bags. He found a group of wooden cases as well but they were identified only by numbers and he was uncertain as to whether they were due to be loaded aboard *Shivandra*. Eventually he left the warehouse, having replaced the oil lamp. He returned to his earlier vantage point and studied the ship once more. Nothing appeared to have changed: the open doorway still glowed brightly although there was no sign of life on the decks.

Striding swiftly across the quay he knelt at one of the mooring bollards and examined the ship's securing ropes carefully. He walked along the dockside, his eyes probing the darkness, seeking details. The sound of a radio pierced the hush of the night and mingled in with the music was the sound of men's voices. Rafferty moved on, finally leaving the freighter behind. He was very thoughtful as he returned to the hotel.

Megan was a late riser and it was only at lunchtime that she met up with her companions once again. After the meal they started their walk along the front of the lagoon accompanied by the faithful Pluto. It was as they came close to *Shi-*

vandra that Dick Rafferty informed his colleagues about his nocturnal walk-about. Megan raised her eyebrows in surprise but the stolid Edwards just smiled slightly.

"If you look at the forward end of the cargo hatch you'll see a small deck-house," he said as they strolled along. "That's where we can gain access to the forward hold. That's going to be the easier hold to hide away in, I think."

As they passed along the length of the steamer Rafferty instinctively glanced up at the bridge but there was no one there. He continued his commentary, explaining that the cargo appeared to be largely coffee and cocoa in sacks.

"You can see that they've started loading already. My guess is that she'll be sailing tomorrow, so if we're going to get aboard it will have to be tonight."

"You haven't said how we are to do that," said Megan evenly.

Rafferty suddenly developed a limp and after a few further paces he hopped to one of the large cast iron mooring bollards. Grimacing theatrically at Pluto, he unlaced his shoe and pretended to search for some foreign body.

"If you look at the ropes you can see that they droop down toward the foc'sle head," he said, all the while smiling at Pluto and sitting with his back to *Shivandra* such that they could easily see over his shoulder. "There are no shields on the hawsers to stop rats getting aboard, and the distance isn't too great. I propose we slide down them and onto the deck. There was no guard posted last night so we shouldn't have a problem."

He replaced his shoe, stood and the party moved off once more.

"Is there no other way aboard?" Megan asked.

Rafferty shook his head understandingly. "I'm afraid not. You see, with a bagged cargo, they load using a net; probably as many as a dozen sacks at a time. There's no way any of us could sneak into the cargo net along with the coffee without being seen. I searched for a large packing case that you might have got inside, just like they do in films, but there simply weren't any of sufficient size in the warehouse. And anyway those that were there may not have been due to be loaded on this ship."

They returned to the hotel and later that evening, over dinner, made detailed plans for stowing away aboard *Shivandra*. Megan reiterated her earlier doubts about being able to negotiate the moorings safely.

"I've thought about that quite a bit," said Rafferty. "I can see the problem, but what I propose is that Edwards, here, carries you."

Megan looked suitably shocked at the suggestion but the big greaser smiled. "Me and Mr. Rafferty have discussed it, Miss. It's only a short way and I reckon I could carry your weight that far. We could mebbe tie you on my back to make it easier."

It all seemed a bit unlikely to Megan but she was acutely conscious that the cargo steamer probably represented their best chance of leaving Grand-Bassam in the short term. She resolved to do her best.

"What time do we leave?" she said by way of reply.

It was agreed that the early hours of the morning would offer the best time at which to board the ship unobserved. Rafferty suggested that they take coffee in the foyer where large circular tables and easy chairs were arranged for that purpose. They reviewed the details of their plans, more as a means of bolstering Megan's confidence than for any other reason. As far as Dick was concerned, the scheme was cut and dried; all he needed now was the cover of darkness for its implementation. The three internees were so deep in conversation that they failed to notice the approach of another European.

It was something of a shock to recognise LeBrun standing smiling at Rafferty's elbow.

"Good," he said enthusiastically, "I find you all together. I have good news for everyone. You will be leaving this splendid place immediately!"

"Leaving!" echoed Megan, abruptly standing up. "But you can't send us away—we're internees."

"I'm afraid my superiors do not agree with you, Miss Baxendell. They feel you would be better looked after elsewhere. You are to board the cargo ship *Shivandra* that sails tonight for Oran that is in Vichy French North African territory. Please be ready to leave the hotel in an hour."

Megan sagged back into her seat defeated. The irony of the situation would strike her later but for the moment she was furious that LeBrun had got the better of her. As the beaming Frenchman strutted away obviously pleased with himself, Rafferty burst out laughing.

"All that effort to find a way aboard and all the time we had only to ask," he said shaking his head.

CHAPTER 20

▼

Arthurian Castle reached the Tunisian coast and turned eastward maintaining a course outside territorial waters. The bow down attitude of the vessel was now becoming noticeable, particularly as the tips of the propeller were beginning to cut the surface with every revolution. This added an unwelcome additional vibration in the shaft that was felt throughout the ship. The level of water in No.1 hold continued to rise despite all efforts to control it by pumping. The matter was becoming serious, as Brian Crawshaw well knew and he paced across the bridge mulling the problem over. It seemed that at the present rate of increase it was just possible that they might make Malta, but it would be a very close run thing with no margin for error. He decided to trust to luck and keep heading for their destination. It had been a fortunate day for the ship with no sightings by the enemy as they had made their slow painful way southwards. The strain was beginning to show already as the under strength crew nursed the stricken merchantman along. Tiredness was evident in men's faces overlaying muscles tensed with concern at their vulnerability. Every man knew that their chances of reaching Malta were slim, particularly now that the Royal Naval escort was no longer there to protect them. It said a lot for their dedication that no one believed that they should abandon their efforts to deliver their cargo to the beleaguered island.

Night arrived with its customary suddenness, but as the moon rose in a cloudless sky visibility was surprisingly clear. Crawshaw had just sighted a light reflecting intermittently across the horizon and was checking it on the chart when he was joined by Fraser McKay and David Watson.

He looked up and nodded. "It seems that the neutral Tunisians still think that there are navigational risks in these waters! That light you can see up ahead seems to be Cape Bon over ten miles away."

"It must be a very powerful beam to be so clear over such a distance," noted David.

"That's true," agreed Crawshaw, "but worse still it's going to light up the old *Arthurian Castle* like a summer's day as we pass it."

"Can't we alter course…go further offshore to avoid it?" grunted McKay.

"Possibly, but it would have to be a huge diversion to be effective and we would be headed for the minefields between here and the island of Pantelleria. I no longer have a chart that's marked with their position, so I'm working by guesswork; but it seems to me the risk is high whichever way we go," replied Crawshaw.

"I suppose that with all that water in No.1 the quicker we get to Malta the better, which presumably means sticking to our present course, eh?" asked McKay grimly.

Just at that moment the conversation was interrupted by a shout from one of the lookouts: "Vessel in sight off the starboard bow!"

The Mate rushed across to the bridge wing, picking up a pair of binoculars from the chart table as he went. He paused, focussing in on a silhouette formed in the moonlight.

"Damn!" he exploded. "Looks like a warship of some sort close inshore." He turned back to the two engineers, looking worried. "She's unlikely to be British; leastwise if she is she shouldn't be inside Tunisian territorial waters."

Crawshaw glanced back to where he had seen the other vessel, his face a picture of concentration. "Damned if he won't see us if we stay on this course," he said at length.

McKay looked across at his colleague meeting his gaze firmly. The big engineer's eyes gradually slid away so that they focussed astern, then returned to the other's face. The Mate held his stare a little longer; then his shoulders sagged slightly as he nodded. He turned to the helmsman and ordered a large helm movement. David, looking out over the sea, watched the bow start to move at an accelerating rate until a further order stopped it as the ship steadied on a new course. Apparently undiscovered, *Arthurian Castle* headed away on the reciprocal of her earlier compass heading, westward along the North African coast.

It was a fateful decision although it would be some time before those onboard became aware of that. They headed west for two hours before it was deemed safe to turn once more for Malta; Crawshaw had calculated the ship's position accurately and the swing eastward was timed to enable them to pass the light at Cape Bon at daybreak in order to avoid its potentially disastrous illumination. As they retraced their original course the atmosphere on the bridge became tense as the ship approached the area of the sighting of the unidentified warship. Crawshaw himself remained, poised with a pair of binoculars to his eyes, out on the wing of the bridge; McKay had stayed in the wheelhouse when David Watson had returned to the engineroom to stand his watch. It came as a mind numbing shock to identify the same ship in apparently the same position in the grey pre-dawn light as it had occupied the previous night. He stared aghast, listening to the lookouts reporting their sighting of the dark hull. He started to turn away from the steel rail, then paused as a thought struck him. Certainly it was a warship and not unlike some of the Royal Naval vessels he had seen shepherding the convoy. He probed further, using the powerful binoculars; there was something odd about the image seemingly wavering before his eyes as his body swayed slightly to the movement of the deck. He concentrated on the distant masts for a moment before reluctantly accepting the situation.

"Seems I was a bit hasty last night, Chief," he said a trifle despondently as he walked back into the wheelhouse.

McKay raised a querying eyebrow but said nothing.

"'Fraid our 'enemy' was just a hulk…a destroyer that ran aground and was abandoned, I shouldn't wonder. Anyway, she's no threat any longer."

"We couldn't have known. It was the right thing to do, reversing course like that!" said McKay, feeling the other's pain at the turn of events.

There was no reply, just a grunt as *Arthurian Castle* continued on course. It was possible to see the outline of the grounded craft more distinctly as they came abreast of and then passed it: the weary observers on the bridge were not to know that they were looking at the disintegrating remains of *HMS Havoc*, stranded and abandoned on the Tunisian coast some months earlier. It might have been some consolation to Chief Officer Brian Crawshaw to know that he was not the only one to have been misled by a sighting of the wreck.

The arrival of the Savoia Marchetti SM79 bomber shortly thereafter was almost inevitable although something of an anticlimax to the vigilant British seamen. The aeroplane was one of a flight of two that had been despatched from Sicily looking for the retreating escorts and capital ships from the Pedestal convoy; in particular they were seeking a Royal Naval submarine which had been reported as being in the vicinity.

Tenente Vicenzo Pantello had been about to alter course, having reached the edge of his patrol area when he spotted the luckless merchant ship. An inexperienced pilot, Pantello immediately regretted the port engine oil leak that had forced his flight commander to return to base soon after take-off. It was not that he lacked courage so much as a dearth of self-confidence. His training had been to attack submarines with depth charges and indeed his aircraft was equipped with these weapons rather than bombs. Attacking an armed freighter taking avoiding action was, in Pantello's mind, a different matter to dropping his missiles on a vessel intent on diving and escaping into the hidden depths of the Mediterranean. Despite his self-doubt he lined up his twin-engine bomber and pushed the controls forward. The SM79 dropped rapidly toward its quarry; the curved bomb bay doors eased open, increasing the bedlam of sound in the fuselage as the speed built up alarmingly. Pantello held the power dive as long as he dared, acutely aware of the tracer rounds curving up to his cockpit. There was a crash as the clear plastic windows to his right side were shattered. He was suddenly surrounded by a howling gale as the aircraft's forward progress was translated into a 200 miles per hour thrust of air through his cabin. A quick glance to the side registered the slumped corpse of his co-pilot riddled by machine gun bullets. He prayed that his bomb-aimer had survived as he dragged the heavy bomber out of its headlong dive. As the freighter flashed by under his wing tips, Pantello was gratified to feel a slight lurch as the two depth charges were released together. His aim had been to drop them just ahead of the port bow of his target where their shallow set hydrostatic fuses would be most effective. He concentrated on heading away from the ship as more tracer shells reached for his command. Although Pantello did not at first realise the Savoia Marchetti had been hit, the changing sound of the port engine with a bullet firmly lodged in its fuel system soon alerted him. Fuel spurted from a severed pipe and inevitably found its way onto the hot exhaust manifold. The engine already misfiring due to fuel starvation, burst into flames. The pilot stared in horror for several seconds before his training took over and he shut the machine down. He depressed the fire extinguisher button as the feathered propeller slowed to a stop and waited, hardly daring to breathe. Though strongly fanned by the aircraft's speed, the flames abated as the extinguishant took effect and eventually disappeared.

Pantello was so preoccupied by his emergency that he did not see the immediate effects of his attack, but as the SM79 levelled off he nudged his stick slightly to swing the nose. He became excited as, looking back, he saw two huge plumes of spray erupt from the sea alongside the bow of the merchantman. As the water subsided and he could see, for the first time, the full length of the ship, it was noticeable that she was lower in the water forward. Convinced that he had dealt a fatal blow to the British ship and aware that his crippled aircraft would need

nursing back to its base, Pantello set course for Sicily, already in his mind savouring the congratulations of his commanding officer.

High up on the bridge of *Arthurian Castle* Brian Crawshaw watched the
departing, smoking bomber, convinced that his command had come off best in
the encounter. The two depth charges, startlingly huge as they detached from the
light painted underside of the bomber, had struck the sea well to port of the bow
already swinging in the opposite direction in an evasive manoeuvre. Their simul-
taneous explosions caused the ship to heel sharply away from the massive water
disturbance but she steadied back on course almost immediately. Crawshaw was
elated that the ship had survived the attack and that her attacker had been damaged into the bargain. He turned to Fraser McKay, grinning. "He'll not bother us
again in a hurry! Looks as though our gunners did a pretty good job."

"Let's hope he doesn't tell his mates where we are," replied Fraser dourly as the
sound of cheering came from the Oerlikon gunners at their mountings alongside
the bridge.

With both protagonists claiming victory it might have seemed at first sight
that the end result could be regarded as a draw. Unfortunately the old merchant
ship's luck was by now fast running out. The underwater explosions had strained
the already weakened forward hull plating to the extent that the leakage into
No.1 hold increased considerably. *Arthurian Castle* was sinking, yet fate had not
yet finished with her. Unnoticed, the almost forgotten unexploded bomb in the
officer's saloon started to tick as the fuse belatedly began to function. Heavily
barricaded with bagged flour though it was, the violent roll caused when the
depth charges detonated alongside the bow was enough to jar an inch or two of
movement. This disturbance was sufficient: the fuse fired and in a milli-second of
prodigious energy release, the bomb's casing ruptured. The barricade did its job
reasonably well. The saloon was filled with heavy clouds of rapidly swirling flour,
but most of the iron casing fragments were absorbed. The force of the explosion
was absorbed in an upward direction, but unfortunately the downward compo-
nent was not sufficiently controlled. The deck was split as if by a giant tin opener
and debris, driven by the force of the shattering discharge, thrashed through into
the boiler room below.

For an instant the space was filled with the shrill whine of flying shards of
metal. In a strange way the fireman on watch in the boiler-room was lucky. He
was struck by a twisted knot of metal that neatly severed the jugular vein at the
side of his neck. He lapsed into unconsciousness and died quickly, unaware of the
major disaster building around him. The high-pressure fuel line supplying the
burners in the straining boiler was fractured and a black oily sheet expanded rap-

idly from the hole until it fragmented into tiny droplets. The evil smelling fluid coated large areas of the space before striking the hot burner carrier plate on the front of the boiler. Within seconds the whole locality was a burgeoning mass of flame greedily feeding on the continuously leaking fuel oil. The speed of advance of the blaze was astonishing. The entire boiler-room was rapidly engulfed; there would have been no escape for the luckless fireman.

In the adjacent engineroom after the detonation of the bomb, the first indication of its consequences was a drop in the steam pressure as fuel leaked away instead of being burnt to raise steam. David frowned as the engine began to slow slightly. He bent his head to peer through the interconnecting doorway at the boiler-room. He recoiled sharply, repelled by the orange inferno and its blast of heat already encroaching on the engine space. Hastily he slammed the steel door shut, aware that no one could have survived beyond it. Rushing to the telephone, he spun the activating handle in an attempt to contact the bridge; but the instrument was useless, its wiring already burnt through where it traversed the boiler-room on its way upwards.

As it happened, there was no need to advise the occupants of the bridge: flames were already reaching out of the skylight immediately behind the wheelhouse. Crawshaw yelled at the helmsman to turn the ship's head into wind to avoid the fire engulfing the entire bridge structure. The man spun the wheel violently. There was a thudding shudder as the telemotor rammed against its stops but there was no reaction: the ship continued on its course away from the visible coastline. The controlling hydraulic pipework between the wheel and the steering engine down aft had also been routed through the blazing boiler-room. The copper pipes were now little more than molten splashes on their red-hot steel supports, their function forever concluded. The ship began to slow down as the reserves of steam were rapidly consumed, but she would travel some miles yet as her uncontrolled momentum gradually diminished.

Fraser McKay took in at a glance the oily black smoke pouring off the flames dancing from the boiler-room skylight and dashed for the leeward side bridge ladder. Within minutes he was at the entrance to the engineroom, heaving the heavy watertight door open. He peered uncertainly down over the massive cylinders of the propulsion engine. There were no immediate signs of fire so he scrambled down the steep ladders, across intermediate platforms, and was soon standing at the control station on the lowest level well beneath the external waterline.

"What's the score, Wattie?"

"Boiler-room's gone, I think, Chief. Tremendous fire." David nodded toward the door he had so recently slammed shut. Its multi-layered coat of white paint was bubbling and discolouring rapidly before their eyes.

McKay closed his eyes briefly, sickened by what he now knew was inevitable.

"Come on, lad, its time to leave. There's nothing more to be done here. Get all your people out of the engineroom and up to the lifeboat station."

For a while, as he ushered the greasers out of the space, David thought that they were in for a repeat of the previous abandonment of *Arthurian Castle*. He was wrong. Even as he sprinted around to his cabin to warn the recovering Fred Gates, the flames swept free of the burnt boiler-room skylight, lashed across the deck in the grip of the wind and gorged themselves on the wooden framework of the one surviving lifeboat. In an unbelievably short space of time the ship had been transformed from a viable if weakened merchant ship into a dangerous blazing hulk that was slowly sinking. Worse still, means of escape from the holocaust were reduced to just two Carley floats fortunately not yet affected by the fire. The two groups of merchant seamen that had struggled through the previous days to take the ship to Malta were separated and isolated by the conflagration; those on the bridge had no means of reaching the off duty seamen who were gathering in a clear space on the after deck along with David's engineroom party.

CHAPTER 21

▼

Privately David Watson wondered whether things could get worse: the ship was clearly sinking, the increasing angle of the deck was proof of that, and she was powerless, burning, in waters that seemed to belong to the enemy. He watched disinterestedly as the Chief Engineer and two sailors scaled the ladder back to the boat deck. McKay had realised that the only means of escape from the doomed merchantman would be the two Carley floats if they could be released before the spreading fire reached them. Following the destruction of the sole lifeboat, the flames had gained a hold on the wood deck cladding. The starboard side of the boat deck was well ablaze and David realised that McKay would have to be quick if he were to free the float on that side ahead of the conflagration. The ship was now all but stopped in the water as the steam reservoir of the starboard boiler was exhausted. David had deliberately left the engine running, reasoning that as the steam pressure declined so would the fuel leakage that was feeding the fire; there had been no other action that could have been taken in the circumstances. As *Arthurian Castle* slowed, so she began to weathervane into the light wind. This had the effect of pushing the flames along the boat deck as well as across it. The movement was slow and Fraser McKay probably didn't notice the change of direction.

Suddenly a tendril of flame driven by an unruly draught of wind reached out hungrily toward the trio struggling with the float release mechanism. The nearest figure, that of McKay, threw up his hands, in seeming capitulation to the heat, but in reality intending to protect his face, then tumbled to the deck in an untidy heap. David stared, stunned by the rapid turn of events as the main conflagration stole, crackling slightly as it consumed tinder-dry decking planks, toward the recumbent form. The two seamen nursing minor burns seemed unable or unwilling to do anything. David rushed up the ladder and seized McKay's feet, tugging strongly.

"Come on, you two, give me a hand!" he yelled as he struggled.

Galvanised by the firmness of the instruction, the two men came to his assistance and soon the heavy Chief Engineer was lifted to safety. David kneeled beside the unconscious figure laid on a wooden hatch board on the after deck. The whole of McKay's right side had been affected: his face was a contrast of two halves, a pink pulpy mass blackened in places compared obscenely with a healthy sun-tanned cheek and jowl. The dark blue uniform jacket had absorbed some of the heat but David could see some overheated flesh mingled with remnants of material along the length of the right arm. There looked to be some lesser damage to the leg in addition.

A voice spoke from the surrounding group of onlookers; it was Fred Gates, his injured arm protected by a huge white sling.

"We should get 'im into the 'ospital…clean 'im up like."

David nodded absently, his eyes fixed on the conflagration behind Fred. Would the flames get a hold in the accommodation and threaten the safety of the hospital, he wondered. He peered at the injured man and decided the risk was justified. As he straightened up willing hands lifted the hatch board like a makeshift stretcher and carried McKay away.

Unnoticed, the boat deck fire raged on, finally consuming the two Carley floats, the only means of escape from the dying freighter. The initial cause of the blaze, the boiler room fuel leak, had by now effectively exhausted itself as the steam driven fuel pump ground to a halt. But the sun-dried decks of the ship offered plenty of combustible material; wooden rails and planks succumbed easily as the hungry flames spread along steel bulkheads coated with thick layers of once white paint. Yet for all the appalling splendour of the leaping flames, the fire was far from superficial, not just confined to the boat deck even though the flare-up from the boiler space had diminished. The stairways that led up from the various cabins to the bridge were flanked on their aftermost perimeter by the very area within which the fire had started. The sheer heat generated had led to new fires starting in electrical cabling. In practical terms the wheelhouse was isolated. As David Watson, by now a self appointed nurse, struggled to cut away ashy cloth remnants from seared flesh, Brian Crawshaw strode backwards and forwards across the width of the ship, his brow furrowed by concern and frustration.

With no escape possible downwards through the accommodation or aft across a flaming boat deck, he knew that he must organise some means of lowering people down the smooth bridge structure onto the foredeck, which was connected to the after end of the ship by an external passageway. It could only be a matter of minutes before fire flashed where he walked. He gestured to the Bosun.

"Is there any rope near at hand?"

The Bosun was quick to understand what Crawshaw had in mind.

"There's some spare signal halyards, I think. Bit thin, but if we double up they would probably serve. I'll see what's in the flag locker."

There was a surprising amount of cordage available and the resourceful Bosun soon plaited a useful line that was secured to the steering wheel pedestal, then suspended through the smashed window. Crawshaw was pleased to note that it reached to within a few feet of the foredeck. One by one the bridge party strong-armed their way to relative safety down the rope; as Crawshaw, the last to leave, started his descent he could hear the crackle of flames eating away at the wheelhouse door.

The hospital was becoming a stuffy place as David worked away on the still unconscious Chief Engineer, due to the numbers of men who had crowded into the room. It was not so much that they had taken a vicarious interest in the proceedings but rather that the only source of authority left to them was in the hospital and they naturally congregated around this authority, having no idea as to what else to do.

David turned to Gates. "Get everyone out of here, would you, Fred? Set a watch on that fire. I'll need to know if it's likely to affect us in here. You might get someone to scout around the accommodation—see if it has invaded there yet."

There was no dissension as David issued his orders; surprisingly, acceptance seemed quite natural. Soon he was alone with his patient. The wounds were now fully exposed. The right leg was only superficially seared whereas the arm had two nasty burns that leaked a pale fluid through shrivelled remnants of skin. He busied himself cleaning the lesions carefully whilst his mind grappled with the problem represented by McKay's ravaged face. Instinctively he knew that the greatest threat to the man's life came from that area but he was unsure as to what he should do by way of treatment. What am I doing? he thought, a marine engineer playing at doctor on a partially floating death trap. Yet instincts deep within him led him to work hard for the well being of his colleague and friend. He found some antiseptic cream in the medicine locker and was able to dress the injuries on his patient's limbs to his own satisfaction. As he completed tying a bandage just above the elbow, McKay began to show signs of returning consciousness.

There was a loud pain-filled groan as the undamaged eyelid flickered open. A single eye stared vacantly before finally focussing on David's concerned features. No words were spoken but David became aware of the other man's understanding and gratitude before the eye closed as he lapsed once more into unconsciousness.

"'ow's 'e doing?"

David turned to see Gates leaning against the doorframe supporting his damaged arm with his good one.

"I honestly don't know," he said. "I've cleaned him up as best I can but I've no means of knowing how serious the burns are."

"What about 'is face? You gonna bandage that as well?"

"I was just trying to decide what I should do, as it happens," replied David.

"My guess is you should cover up as much of the injury as possible. I remember my schoolmate, Jimmy Perkins, 'e fell in a bonfire one Guy Fawkes Night. They trussed 'im up like an Egyptian mummy an 'e got better all right," said Fred helpfully.

David nodded his acceptance although privately worried as to how to apply a bandage successfully to the burnt flesh.

"Yer quite the doctor aren't you?" murmured Fred. "First me, now 'im."

"It's not by choice, believe me," replied David, "but I can't just leave my shipmates to suffer!"

"No, exactly," said Fred quietly as he left the hospital.

When Gates returned to the deck he was greeted by the Mate, Crawshaw leading a group of seamen.

"Where's Mr. McKay?"

Fred explained what had happened and ushered the deck officer toward the hospital. David was struggling with a swathe of bandages that circled the Chief Engineer's head. The injured man was semi-conscious and twisting around on the medical bed in obvious pain. Crawshaw used his weight to gently restrain the writhing body whilst David finished off.

"Have you given him any morphine?" asked Crawshaw.

"No, I haven't found any in the medicine cabinet. Besides, I'm not sure whether I could inject it."

"Don't worry, if I remember rightly we should have some in tablet form," replied Crawshaw as he rummaged in the locker. "Ah! Here we are. Let's try him with one of these."

In a surprisingly short time the drug took affect and the bandaged form relaxed seemingly into a deep sleep. Crawshaw nodded in satisfaction, then beckoned David out of the room.

"We'd better take stock of the situation. I take it the engineroom is finished?"

David shrugged. "The fire started in the boiler-room after the bomb exploded; it could only have been caused by fuel oil, probably a ruptured pipe. Whatever the cause, the boiler-room will have been wiped out in the inferno. Without steam for the pumps there's no way of extinguishing such a large fire." He gestured toward the flames remorselessly eating their way across the boat deck. "We just have to hope it burns itself out!"

"No chance of that I'm afraid," replied Crawshaw. "It's already in the accommodation. We were nearly trapped on the bridge."

"So what chance do we have?" asked David. "Wait for the ship to burn out, or maybe she'll sink first?" He was aware of the hopelessness in his voice as he spoke, but the strain-induced tiredness of the last few hours was beginning to settle on him like a heavy weight, sapping his will.

Crawshaw smiled grimly. "Let's get some food and have a rest. Things might not look quite so black afterwards. I think the safest place would be right aft in the steering flat well away from the fire. We'd best move the Chief whilst he's reasonably comfortable."

David looked gratefully at the older man, thankful for the encouragement in his words. He set about organising the transfer of his patient, once again making use of the makeshift stretcher. For his part Crawshaw gave orders for a hot meal to be prepared and food to be stockpiled in the safe haven around the steering engine. Mattresses were brought and soon the space was made reasonably comfortable for the fifteen surviving crewmembers.

The ship drifted through the night borne on a south-westerly current but held well clear of the land by an offshore breeze. There was little that could be done and most spent the time sleeping. McKay was kept sedated with the morphine tablets administered at intervals; David tended him as best he could, conscious of his inability to do more to hasten the man's recovery.

At daybreak he made his way back onto the deck and regarded the surrounding sea moodily. Despite a decent rest he could find no glimmer of optimism in his soul. They were still trapped aboard the foundering hulk of a once proud ocean-going merchant ship with smears of smoke issuing from various parts of her superstructure. True, the bow did not feel as though it were any deeper in the water, but it could only be a matter of time before further bulkheads failed and the vessel took her final short voyage to the sea bed. He was joined at the rail by Crawshaw.

"Things look any brighter this morning?"

David smiled despite himself. "You mean the situation's changed?"

"Well, normally, if one sleeps on a problem it doesn't look quite so bad in the fresh light of day!"

"Do you have any magic solutions?"

Crawshaw peered grimly at David. "No, I'm afraid not. How far can you swim?"

"Surely the question is: 'How far can the Chief swim?', I would have thought," replied David in a low voice.

"You're an odd one, Wattie," observed Crawshaw as he turned away from the rail and made his way toward the smoking structure in the middle of the ship.

David stood for a while longer looking out over the featureless blue sea, unconsciously searching within himself for some spark of hope. His concentration focussed on the distant horizon and he became unaware of his immediate surroundings. Suddenly and for no apparent reason he thought of his promise to see Megan in London, made at the time of the sinking of *Petrain Castle*. An image of her huddled on the thwart of the lifeboat bore in on the front of his consciousness. He indulged himself in a private fantasy in which he kept such an appointment.

He stood motionless at the ship's rail, oblivious to the passage of time; then it came to him that at that moment the most important thing in the world to him was to get back to London and hope that Megan managed to do the same. He stood back from the rail, his shoulders a little squarer, his stance a little straighter. It was time to get on with things, he decided, as he returned to the steering flat.

"How's that arm of yours, Fred?" he enquired as he confronted his pal sitting on a mattress cuddling a cup of steaming coffee.

"Aches a bit, 'specially if I knock it on anything," came the honest reply.

"It must be time I changed the dressing. Give me a minute to grab a bite to eat and I'll be with you."

David spent the next hour in his newly adopted nursing role, attending first to Fred Gates and then Fraser McKay. He was even approached by the two seamen who had also been slightly burned on the boat deck and who asked him to treat their wounds. The last clean bandage was just being tied off when Crawshaw re-entered the space. He motioned to David, pointing up the short stairway to the after deck.

They resumed their earlier positions at the rail looking seaward.

"How are the invalids?" asked the Mate without preamble.

David paused, marshalling his thoughts. "Gates is healing, I think. I've changed the dressing and the wound seems to be free of infection, as far as I can tell. He's a strong lad so I'm not too worried. The Chief's another matter altogether. I really don't know what I'm doing. The leg and arm should be fine, but his face is a real mess and he's developed a bit of a temperature. The morphine keeps him quiet and pain free but he needs a proper doctor as soon as possible."

"Hmm, I guessed you might say something like that," replied Crawshaw thoughtfully. "I've had a good scout around up forward. The fire's got a firm hold in the cabin area but the bow seems to be no lower in the water; perhaps all those drums of aviation spirit are providing a bit of buoyancy, I don't know."

"You didn't find any spare lifeboats kicking around, did you?" asked David mischievously.

Crawshaw ignored the irony. "No…but I'm damned if I'm going to sit around whilst this old tub sinks under us. I've got some ideas—see what you think."

The Mate outlined his plan in a few quick sentences, then stood back awaiting a reply. He was pleasantly surprised by David's brief, enthusiastic, "Let's do it!"

CHAPTER 22

▼

The plan was at once both simple and obvious; Crawshaw had realised that the ship was drifting close to land and could be expected to ground somewhere along the Tunisian coast once the wind direction changed. It followed logically that some form of raft would be needed to ferry the survivors through the surf and onto the beach. His proposal to David Watson had involved scavenging within the cargo holds to find suitable material from which to manufacture a raft. They would require lifting tackle, which was stored in the engineroom, as the cargo winches were useless without steam to drive them.

David sought out Steve Orme to help him and together they disappeared into the burning accommodation block. It was the quickest way of reaching the engineroom and they moved carefully. Even in the alleyways adjacent to the deck there were still thin streamers of smoke wafting along. The area was heavily redolent of strange burning smells: the acrid taint of ravaged paintwork, the more pleasant aroma of smouldering wood and the pungent tang of rubber cable insulation all combined to assail the senses. The heat from the unseen fire brought an immediate sheen of perspiration to the faces of the two engineers as they moved warily toward the steel engineroom door.

"Careful, Steve, the fire may have broken through from the boiler room," muttered David as the other reached for the cast iron dogs securing the door.

"The door feels reasonably cool," replied Orme as he slowly eased the heavy metal plate back against its hinges.

The engine room was strangely still with no machinery turning in its gloomy depths that were scarcely penetrated by the weak sunlight filtering down from the skylights. There was an eerie quality about the space, it seemed to David, more used to the ear-battering din that normally greeted his entry. The fire had remained in the boiler space, moving upwards as it fed on anything inflammable.

"At least there's no sign of flame," said David cautiously. "Let's get down to the store and out again as quickly as possible."

There was no threat to their safety as they descended the ladders and in minutes they were sorting through a variety of multi-sheaved rope blocks.

"Shall we take a couple of chain blocks as well?" asked Orme.

David shook his head. "Too heavy…we'll be able to lift most things with the rope pulley blocks."

They carried the lifting tackle up to the entrance doorway, then retraced their steps to collect a variety of shackles and strops in addition. Orme made the first trip out to the deck with a pile of gear.

The fire was by now gradually working through the various cabins and public rooms. Unseen, it greedily ate away at the door to the Chief Steward's room; it had already shattered the glass of the two portholes and the rush of air through the apertures whipped the blaze into renewed fury. The heavy wooden door staunchly resisted the onslaught but inevitably it was consumed and bright orange flames burst into the passageway running alongside the engineroom. The heavy paint encrustation, the result of years of regularly applied coatings, bubbled and discoloured, then burst alight. The flame front moved with astonishing speed to engulf the whole area.

The sudden reappearance of the conflagration almost caught out the two engineers: Orme had returned for another load and David was helping to lift a heavy block when the flame front crackled past the open doorway. The hot breath of fire frizzled his eyebrows as he slammed shut the door. Orme yelped as the sleeve of his boiler suit ignited; he frantically beat at his arm, then peered suspiciously at the charred smoking hole in his overall.

"Okay?" queried David.

Orme nodded without conviction, his face chalky white and covered with a greasy sheen. "How the hell are we going to get out of here? We're trapped!" His voice cracked close to panic.

David reached out and plucked at the burn on his friend's overall, seemingly ignoring the exclamation. The brief contact steadied Orme. "Another good boiler suit ruined," he observed at length.

"Come on," said David, "we'd best get down to the shaft tunnel. We can use the emergency escape at the stern gland up to the steering flat."

Orme's lips twisted in a sheepish grin. He had forgotten about the special trunking situated right aft where the propeller shaft penetrated the hull. He followed his partner down the steel flights until they were both standing on the lowest platform alongside the huge structure of the silent propulsion engine. The thin light filtering down from the skylights scarcely provided any illumination and David was obliged to use the torch. There was the sound of swishing water as the ship rolled slowly. Without steam to operate the pump the bilges were gradually filling with wastewater; there was already a couple of feet of oily fluid surging around beneath their feet.

Although not of itself serious, the water served as a reminder of the risk to their safety posed by the flooding in the forward cargo hold. David forced himself to ignore the association of ideas.

"Looks as if we can ignore the fire!" he offered, smiling broadly.

Orme looked mystified.

"Yeah, I reckon we'll sink first," continued David. They both laughed at the weak attempt at a joke and the tension relaxed slightly.

"Come on," added David as he set off toward the aftermost engineroom bulkhead.

There was a large cast-iron watertight door set against the steel; it was closed. Orme seized a bulky four-spoked handwheel and heaved. The door was moved by a cog engaging with teeth formed in its edge. The handwheel operated the gear but it had jammed. David added his strength but to no avail.

He stepped back, wiping droplets of sweat from his eyes. "This is ridiculous. It was only closed the other day during the first attack. It can't be badly jammed."

They tried again with no appreciable effect.

"Hang on, I'll get a wheel spanner." David dashed back to the control position and seized a claw shaped device with a long handle. This enabled them to get a better purchase on the recalcitrant wheel. It began to turn. The door inched open. They redoubled their efforts and soon an eighteen-inch gap was established but then it jammed once more.

"Hold up, let's take a breather," gasped a puffing Orme.

They sat together looking through the narrow gap at the long length of the propeller shaft, shiny in the light of their torch, stretching into the darkness.

"What do you think of our chances? You know…getting off the ship…getting rescued…whatever." Orme was clearly rattled.

David tried a reassuring smile, aware of his own lack of conviction. "We should be alright providing we can get the raft built before we take in any more water up for'ard." He paused as a new thought struck him. "Mind you, I'm not sure what happens when we get ashore. Maybe there are Germans over there."

Orme looked aghast. "You mean, we'll become prisoners of war? But I'm a civilian, for goodness sake!"

"Somehow I don't think being a civilian will help," said David grimly. "Come on, let's get out of here."

For an instant it appeared as though Steve Orme was going to continue the discussion but any comment he might have made was forgotten as a deep ominous thud reverberated strongly through the very fabric of the ship. It was followed by a gushing noise reminiscent of the sound of a bath being emptied but without the gurgle. The deck beneath their feet noticeably tilted; David grabbed a section of pipework to avoid sliding forward.

"Sounds like No1 hold bulkhead finally threw in the towel," he observed laconically.

Turning back to the watertight door he found Orme already squeezing himself through the partial opening. He shrugged and followed his colleague. They emerged into a narrow passage with a semi-circular upper surface. They could just stand upright on the restricted walkway if they remained one behind the other. The space was dominated by the heavy propeller shaft and its huge connecting flanges. They moved slowly towards the stern. The torch cast an eerie orange glow that bounced off white painted railings, weighty bearings and the shaft. David glanced upward, imagining the weight of cargo just above their heads. He cursed as the moment's lack of concentration caused him to stumble. Finally they reached the end of the tunnel. They were in a wider space where it was possible to see the shafting entering the gland that held the outside sea at bay and beyond which hung the huge manganese bronze propeller. The gland leaked slightly, causing a splashing of water at the after bulkhead. Normally they would have been well below the surface of the sea at this point but David suspected that with the ship sinking by the bow a fair proportion of the propeller would now be above the surface.

He flashed the torch beam around seeking the escape trunk. He almost missed the steel rungs welded to the bulkhead.

"You first, Steve."

Orme needed no second invitation and was soon clambering laboriously up the vertical ladder. He disappeared into a section of trunking, a sort of square pipe only to reappear after a few seconds.

"It's as black as hell in here," he said in a rather plaintive tone. "I can't see to release the upper hatch dogs."

Without a word David handed him the torch. Within seconds he found himself in the pitch dark as Orme climbed away. There was a moment of panic but he forced himself to remain calm. His imagination began to lead his mind astray as time expanded. Every tiny sound vibrating through the gently rolling hull was magnified. Was the deck beginning to incline further? Was that more water bursting in up forward? Suddenly he heard a muffled shout and saw a slight lightening of the stygian blackness in the region of the ladder. He grasped a rung and swung himself up. Above his head was a faint light that steadily strengthened as he moved upwards. Eventually he reached a small aperture through which he squeezed to find himself back in the steering flat. He took a deep breath as Orme and Fred Gates helped him to stand up, more relieved to be back with his fellow survivors than he cared to admit.

"Welcome 'ome," said Gates cheerfully. "The Mate said you'd come back this way. What with the fire an' all."

It didn't seem to have occurred to Fred that the two engineers might have sustained injury in the sudden extension of the fire.

"They're up by No.4 'old working on a raft," he added helpfully.

"How's Mr. McKay?"

"No change as far as I can tell."

David went over to where the Chief Engineer lay. He felt a sweat-streaked brow, aware that the fever remained, and frowned. The sooner he could get his patient professional help the better, even if it had to be from a German doctor. He followed Gates out onto the deck and was soon helping the raft-making team.

The limited amount of lifting tackle that Orme had removed from the engineroom before the fire had claimed the access passageway was being used, suspended from a derrick, to lift drums of petrol from the hold. There was an amount of aviation spirit in each hold but that in No.4 hold was the most accessible. A team of seamen was hauling on a rope as David approached. He joined in and before long a large black barrel swayed over the coaming around the hold. It was manhandled to the ship's side and a cap in its upper surface was unscrewed. As it was tipped and emptied over the side, David noticed Brian Crawshaw striding along the deck toward him, beckoning.

"You'd better have a look at this," he said without explanation.

He retraced his steps down the slope of the deck in the direction of the bow with David struggling to match his long legged stride. They passed the smoking fire-damaged accommodation block and emerged on the foredeck. Despite himself, David was astonished. The foc'sle head was now under water, the huge gear wheels of the anchor windlass creating two humped metallic islands in the gently rolling sea. Behind them the Mediterranean lapped regularly over the tarpaulin covering the bomb damage to No.2 hold. It was clear that the cargo area was filling with seawater. But it was not the immersion of the forepart of the ship that served to surprise, after all that had begun with the torpedo boat attack. It was the deck plating immediately in front of the rearing steel of the superstructure. The escape rope from the bridge still swung untended over the gaping hole left by the bomb that had penetrated the officer's saloon. The breach was scarcely worsened by the explosion of the bomb, given the protection afforded by the flour sacks, but their defence had not extended to floor level. The massive rent that had been the precursor to the boiler room fire had extended forward into the riveting where the saloon bulkhead was secured to the main deck. Aided by unnoticed long-term corrosion of the metal, the split had spread across the ship along the line of the rivets. Whether the damage would have been terminal without the concomitant hold flooding is debatable, as it was the tremendous weight of water inundating the cargo that served as a colossal lever. The bomb-fractured deck was being gradually ripped apart. David could see a gap of more than a foot in width extending into the ship's side. Even in the slight swell that was running, the two halves of the scar were moving sufficiently to cause a tooth-jangling screech as they ground together.

David could scarcely comprehend the significance of the ruined deck. He turned to the Mate, "What's going to happen?"

Crawshaw grimaced. "I'm not really sure, to be honest. With luck, and providing that the boiler room bulkhead holds, we should be fairly safe down aft. By which I mean the ship will continue to float...we're not far from the coast, so providing a raft can be built we should be able to get ashore. The problem is if the weather deteriorates; even a minor storm could force the bow backwards. Once the engine and boiler rooms flood I'm afraid the old *Arthurian* has had it!"

He gestured to the submerged part of the ship, then looked up at the sky as if seeking inspiration.

"We need a slice of luck. If you have a God I suggest you pray to him now!"

They wandered slowly up the steep slope of the deck. There were now three petrol drums ranged against the ship's rail with a fourth in the final stages of clearing the hold. A strong smell of petrol hung over the whole area despite the light wind that teased at the men's shirts.

"Just as well we're clear of the accommodation fire here on the after deck," observed David.

Crawshaw nodded. "Mind you, I think the blaze has just about exhausted itself. There's still lots of smoke but I haven't seen any flame in the last half-hour. You can even get back into the engineroom if you want. Wear gloves, though—everywhere is still very hot."

During the afternoon the raft began to take shape under the watchful eye of the Bosun: it was a simple structure comprising a lattice of wooden hatch covers lashed together and supported at each corner by a petrol drum. It was finished by nightfall and the discussion in the steering flat as the evening meal was consumed centred on the timing of its future use. Crawshaw refused to be drawn on the matter.

During the long night the Mate made frequent visits to the deck where he stood staring out to starboard hopefully. It was shortly after two in the morning that his vigil was rewarded; a faint ribbon of light was visible intermittently on the distant unseen horizon. At first he was hopeful that it would be the lighthouse at Cape Bon, the same beacon that had been visible as they skirted the Tunisian coast before the Italian bomber had found them. He quickly realised that it was a weaker source and guessed that it was rotating at a slower rate. The ship must be drifting at a faster rate than he would have expected, he decided, but he was encouraged nonetheless. Quite clearly *Arthurian Castle* would drive ashore within the day. He decided to get some rest while the opportunity was available.

A few hours sleep revived Crawshaw and he felt refreshed as he lay on a mattress looking up at the rivets in the deckhead above him. Then the movement of the ship registered and he knew what had woken him. He jumped to his feet still dressed but shrugging into a coat whilst his feet searched for his shoes. He scrambled up to the deck once more, trying not to wake those around him. Out on the poop deck it was instantly apparent that the wind had shifted and strengthened. To make matters worse, it was raining heavily and he was soon drenched to the skin, shivering as the warmth was drained from his body. He plodded into the wind down the forward slope of the deck until he was again standing in front of the bridge as he had done earlier with David Watson.

The ship was rolling more heavily but not dangerously so. What caused him to purse his lips and shake his head in a gesture of hopelessness was the movement of the bow—or more exactly, that of the immediately visible area of foredeck given that the bow was already under water and in any event hidden in the darkness. He shone his torch out over the sea and was appalled as a white crested wave loomed over No.2 hatch coaming, then smashed down thunderously. The frightening thing was not the impact of the wave but the fact that the front of the ship made no effort to rise to the undulation of the sea. He knew that there was no reserve buoyancy left forward of the accommodation with which the old ship could combat the increasing swell, but he tasted the acidity of fear in his mouth as he realised that she could not take much pounding in deteriorating weather. The freighter would sink soon and without warning. He paused, surveying the scene a little longer. There was no doubt about it—the wind strength was still increasing. He swung the torch along the crack in the steel deck. It was appreciably wider. There was also a groaning noise emanating from the overstressed metal as it twisted to the action of the waves. He stumbled back up the deck toward the relative safety of the steering flat but was met by a shadowy figure hunched against the driving rain.

"How does it look?" shouted David, combating the howl of the wind.

"Not good."

"Is it time for the raft?" persisted David.

"In this weather! Look over the side!" Crawshaw waved the beam of the torch over the whitened sea, shaking his head. "Too rough…if it didn't capsize whilst we were launching, we'd never get everyone aboard."

David thought of Fraser McKay fighting the fevers of his body in a semiconscious state and recognised the truth of Crawshaw's assessment.

"For the time being we can only sit out the storm and hope," said the Mate sadly. "I think we would be safer up on deck. When she goes it will be quick."

Over the next half an hour the survivors congregated in the vicinity of the raft. They all wore life jackets and a variety of coverings from heavy coats to sections of tarpaulin in an effort to preserve some element of protection from the pouring rain. David organised the carrying of McKay up from the steering flat and had him placed on the raft. It seemed only natural to lash the stricken engineer in place. Fred Gates joined David and McKay on the wooden surface. He dragged a sheet of canvas with him and soon the three men were sheltered from the worst of the weather. David waved to Crawshaw but the Mate was occupied with the other survivors and did not see the gesture.

The storm built steadily as the night wore on. Somehow, and against the odds, *Arthurian Castle* managed to fight her way through to the weak light of dawn. Mercifully the rain died away but everyone was frozen to the marrow by that time. It was possible to see the waves as they rushed in on the struggling hull. The foredeck was now completely under the surface and the curling breakers smashed themselves against the front of the bridge, sending huge showers of spray high into the air. It was clear to David that the boiler room had begun to flood: it was equally apparent that the ship was close to her end. He glanced out to starboard and was vaguely surprised to see a ribbon of land. It was impossible to judge distance but he knew it was further than he could swim.

He was still staring at the distant shore, willing the ship to stay afloat for just a little while longer, when it happened. The Tyne-siders who had built the vessel had done their job well. Despite the massive buffeting of the waves, the bow held in place, attached by a diminishing hinge of failing steel. Unfortunately it was now over thirty feet deeper in the water than it should have been. There was a colossal thump and a heavy vibration resonated through the frames of the ship as she struck an outlying cluster of rocks.

David clung onto McKay as *Arthurian Castle* stopped in her tracks, then began to slew around across the wind. There was an agonising screech of tortured metal from somewhere up forward. Oddly the ship settled onto a more even keel giving a false sense of normality. There was another great crash from within the bowels of the ship. David realised that the sea was now much nearer to the rails—they were sinking. There was a cry off to his left. He turned in time to see a bulky figure sliding between two iron stanchions and over the side into a murderous looking sea. He realised that the broken hull had taken on a list. The raft slid slightly before jamming against a pair of heavy mooring bitts. There was the feeling of movement across his body as Gates dragged the piece of canvas more closely around the recumbent form between them. A tremendous comber tore toward them, smashing into the deck just feet away. The deck was now largely under water and men were floating away unable or unwilling to hold on longer. Soon the only occupants of the deck were the three men clinging to the raft. The ship sank even lower. It was then that David saw that they were not floating; the raft was held by the sinking vessel, as if she were determined to take her cargo with her to the grave. A flutter of panic twisted his stomach as he wildly looked around him, seeking some means of freeing their craft. Then for the first time that fateful night the storm came to their aid. A particularly venomous wave expended its energy directly on top of them, driving breath from lungs and nearly drowning them all before it receded. But the very weight of water was sufficient to dislodge the raft, which drifted away from the wreck rapidly.

David gaped at Gates, seeing his fear reflected in the other man's eyes. The storm continued to rage, tossing the tiny float and its three-man cargo to and fro like a wolf worrying its prey. Life became simply a continuous fight to maintain contact with a few square feet of wood lashed to some empty barrels. Struggling, as he himself was, David would wonder for the rest of his life how Fred Gates managed to survive with only one reliable arm with which to grasp the rope lashings. The fight for survival left neither man aware that the raft was approaching the shore. It came as a further shock to nervous systems that had already absorbed too much when the oil drums suddenly bumped on a sandy bottom. Their uncontrolled motion checked for an instant before a following wave picked them up and hurled them up the beach. It proved to be a farewell gesture and they lay there on their raft like flotsam. It was a luxury to remain in one place without having to fight to stay there. Somehow over-stressed bodies knew the immediate danger was passed and David and Fred fell asleep. McKay mumbled in his drugged state, mercifully unaware of the events that had surrounded him.

CHAPTER 23

▼

The taste of sand was gritty in his mouth as he awoke. David forced his eyes open against the salt encrustation and gazed along a long white expanse of a broad beach. The storm had moved on taking its malevolence to some distant part of the coastline. A small swell lapped at the drum floats of the raft, which were now partially buried in the sand as a result of wave action. David sat up slowly, aware of aching muscles overstressed in the desperate struggle for survival of the previous night. Gates remained asleep, his scrawny chest moving rhythmically, his features untroubled in the morning sunlight. Somewhat to his surprise, David realised that Fraser McKay was awake also; he found himself staring into a single clear intelligent eye.

"How do you feel, Chief?" he asked.

"Not so bad." The reply was made with evident difficulty as the movement of the mouth pulled at the seared skin of one side of McKay's face.

"How's the pain…I brought some morphine if it's too bad. Just blink your good eye a couple of times if you want a tablet."

The bandaged face before him remained motionless although David thought he detected a hint of Stoicism in the undressed eye. In a few brief sentences he explained the sequence of events that had led to the three of them being there on the deserted beach. Then he stood up to gaze around. He was immediately aware of a dull ache in his left leg. Unexpectedly the cloth of his trousers was shredded below the knee and a nasty gash contrasted redly with the whiteness of his flesh. Ignoring the pain, he struggled up the beach toward a thin line of coarse grass. The distance was no more than twenty yards but the sheer softness of the sand meant that his feet were enveloped at every step. He arrived panting at the patch of greenery. Disappointingly, there was little to see. The landscape was flat and sandy, disappearing into a dull haze in the distance. Patches of grass relieved the sun burnt whiteness at intervals and to one side there was a length of general flatness that could have been a track of some sort.

As he scrutinised the view he noticed a cloud of dust away to his left. It became apparent that the disturbance was moving. David's first instinct was to hide, but then he remembered McKay's injuries. He stood still as the cloud resolved itself into a small truck sliding about slightly as it scudded across the sand. It pulled up alongside him and four soldiers jumped down from the bed of the vehicle. A rifle was brandished at him, accompanied by a splurge of unintelligible words. In an act of discretion David raised his hands above his head. It seemed to be the required reaction and the speaker relaxed somewhat yet kept his gun raised. The door of the truck grated open noisily and a tall neatly dressed man appeared from around the radiator. He was clearly an officer although David did not recognise the insignia on the dark olive green uniform.

The soldier regarded Watson curiously for a few moments before speaking. "British Merchant Navy?" he enquired courteously.

David nodded without comment.

"What ship?"

For some reason it seemed incorrect to reveal this information. David simply smiled without comment.

The officer shrugged as if the matter was of little interest. He looked past the engineer at the raft and the two figures lying there. A few sharp words despatched the four soldiers down the beach. They returned slowly shepherding Gates who was desperately supporting the weight of McKay. The Chief Engineer was making a gallant attempt at walking, but it was clearly too much for him. Twice he fell, twice Gates pulled him upright once more. They struggled on flanked by the unhelpful soldiery until McKay thankfully subsided on the grass near David.

The officer examined the Chief's bandages, then gave orders for him to be lifted into the back of the lorry. The other two survivors were ushered into place alongside the recumbent form; the soldiers took up seats adjacent to the tailboard and the vehicle lumbered off, retracing its outward journey. David's watch had ceased to function sometime during the night but he estimated that they were travelling for over an hour, most of it along well-finished roads, before pulling into a broad driveway. They were outside a wide single storey building fabricated from stone resplendent in a pristine coat of whitewash. It looked for all the world like some bigwig's mansion to David but his first impression was proven wrong as two uniformed nurses swept down the steps from the imposing entry doorway.

They examined McKay gently, then a string of orders was issued. A stretcher appeared and the big man was carried carefully into the hospital. Watson and Gates followed after a quick glance at the officer had elicited a nod.

Later that day the two friends sat in individual beds discussing their situation. They had had their various wounds cleaned and freshly dressed and were resting in a small side ward filled with just four beds. The only discordant note was provided by the swarthy soldier sitting, his rifle cradled in his arms, just outside the entrance to the room.

"Wonder where Chiefy is," commented Fred Gates at one point.

"Judging by our experiences, he's getting medical attention," observed David. "I must say I'm glad we struck lucky in being brought here. I don't think Mr. McKay would have survived much longer on board *Arthurian Castle*. I didn't really know what to do for him for the best."

There was the sound of voices at the door and two soldiers appeared carrying a stretcher. Soon Fraser McKay was made comfortable in a third bed. His dressings were new but just as voluminous as those David had applied.

"He should be fine, given time," said a clear confident voice in accented English.

David swivelled in his bed to regard one of the nurses that had greeted them on their arrival. A tall dark middle-aged woman returned his stare through steel rimmed spectacles. She radiated an aura of authority and David guessed that her word was law in the small establishment.

"Thank you, madam," said David formally.

"The doctor on your ship did a good job binding the burns. There will be some disfigurement, of course, but we seem to have avoided the major infection that usually causes problems in these cases."

David made no comment although secretly pleased by the nurse's words. He shook his head at Gates who seemed about to say something.

"What about our injuries?" he asked.

"Your leg will heal quickly. We'll change the dressings daily; meanwhile you should rest it. As for your friend here," she smiled at Gates, "I'm afraid things will take a little longer. There's some infection around the stitching but do not worry, we will make sure you get better."

Gates returned the smile. "Where exactly are we, Sis?"

The white uniformed figure hesitated a fraction at the mode of address, then ignored it. "Did not Lieutenant Varincourt explain? This is the Vichy French territory of Algeria. We are not far from the town of Bone."

With that she swept out of the ward with a rustling of crisply starched material.

"Well, what do you know! 'ow about that then!" exclaimed Gates excitedly. Then his face fell as a thought struck him; "'ang on, Vichy French? Aren't they the mob wot's in with the Nazis?"

"'Fraid so," replied David. "The question is, are there any Germans around here?"

In practice they had faired better then their shipmates, most of whom had landed in nearby Tunisia. Fortunately all had survived the shipwreck, to be taken to internment camps near Sfax. A notable exception was Chief Officer Brian Crawshaw who, alone in the turbulent sea, had been spotted by the alert lookout of a patrolling Italian motor torpedo boat. He was picked up and after being landed was eventually sent to Germany where he sat out the rest of the war in a prisoner of war camp outside Bremen, Marlag und Milag Nord.

David spent a week at the little hospital before being taken to an internment camp where he joined various other European nationals, civilians like himself who were trapped in the country through no fault of their own. There were also more survivors of the convoy whose ships had been sunk. Over the months of his incarceration David was able to piece together much of the story of the Malta convoy known as Pedestal. Of the merchantmen that left the Clyde, only five reached Malta and discharged their cargoes; fortunately for the beleaguered island's defenders one of the survivors was a tanker, Ohio. The Royal Navy lost ships and men as well, but despite the appalling cost the convoy was a success. The island, thus reprovisioned, was able to retake the offensive: standing as it did across the supply routes to the German forces in North Africa, its strategic importance was immeasurable. The German offensive ground to a halt and fighting in the area ceased. The next convoy to Malta arrived at its destination virtually unscathed. The sacrifices, the heroism of Pedestal, were shown not to have been in vain.

The time David spent in Laghouat Camp outside Algiers was the dreariest of his life. Sited in the desert not far from Algiers, the internment establishment was an old Beau Geste style fort based about a Saharan oasis. There was nothing particularly to do and little hope of a change in the situation whilst the war continued. The one bright spot in a miserable period was the arrival of a fit again Fred Gates. It was only with his friend's arrival that David realised how much he had missed the irrepressible Cockney. They were treated well as internees despite being confined to the camp. The restriction was irksome but in truth any escape was virtually impossible, given the expanse of desert that surrounded them. They managed to glean news of the war from the guards, but even so, it came as a surprise when, one bright November morning, a line of strange lorries approached Laghouat.

They were American, part of an army that had landed earlier. The camp inmates had scarcely finished thanking their saviours and celebrating their release before they were transported to the coast.

CHAPTER 24

▼

"Did you think the trip in *Arthurian Castle* would end up like this, Fred?" asked David.

"'ell no," growled Gates. "Thank God we survived—there's many as didn't!"

"You know, nothing will ever be quite the same again. We've seen so much, experienced so much."

"Amen to that," replied the Cockney.

They were standing at the rail of a large passenger ship steaming rapidly through the Bay of Biscay. The weather was foul and there were only a few hardy souls that had braved the elements to pace the deck. For David the freedom represented by the fresh air was vastly superior to the crowded areas below despite the chill north-easterly wind and occasional rain-filled squall. The experiences of the internment camp were not easy to forget even though they had lasted no more than three months.

"I see Chiefie made it," continued Gates. "'e's on his feet as well down in the sick bay."

David grinned, happily surprised. "You don't say! That's great! I'll go and look him up later."

They stood chatting comfortable in each other's company until it was time for their evening meal. As they turned away from the rail, Gates paused as if struck with a sudden thought.

"The question is: will you ship out again after yer survivors leave?"

David looked at him curiously before answering quietly, "Of course."

The weather improved as they entered the Irish Sea and more people took to strolling the decks, each seeking a first sight of British shores. The liner's course denied them that until approaching the Isle of Arran at the entrance to the Firth of Clyde on the way to a berth in Glasgow.

There was a group of women, also ex-internees of the Vichy French, amongst the motley collection of passengers. As it happened, they were clustered at the ship's side for the first time since leaving Oran, when Arran came abeam. They were chattering excitedly and David laughed at their enthusiasm for this first manifestation of home. Standing some yards away he could not hear what was being said but there was a gaiety about the group that he found appealing. As he watched them he began to sense a certain familiarity about one of the girls. He continued to stare at one particular individual who seemed to feel his gaze. She turned and he felt his heart bound as confusion and disbelief enveloped his mind.

Megan walked slowly over to him, smiling softly. "Looks like we won't have to wait until we get to London," she murmured as their fingers touched lightly.

978-0-595-36665-1
0-595-36665-1

Printed in the United Kingdom
by Lightning Source UK Ltd.
105935UKS00001B/235-246